I0567455

GIVE ME EVERYTHING

by

Angela Kay Austin

Vanilla Heart Publishing
USA

Give Me Everything
by Angela Kay Austin

Copyright 2012 Angela Kay Austin

Published by: Vanilla Heart Publishing
www.VanillaHeartBooksAndAuthors.com
10121 Evergreen Way, 25-156
Everett, WA 98204 USA

All rights reserved. No part of this book may be reproduced or transmitted in any form or by any means, electronic or mechanical, including photocopying, recording or by any information storage and retrieval system without written permission from the publisher, except for the inclusion of brief quotations in a review.

This book is a work of fiction. Names, characters, places, and incidents are either the product of the author's imagination or are used fictitiously, and any resemblance to places, events, or persons living or dead is purely coincidental.

ISBN-13: 9780692021408 ISBN-10: 069202140X

10 9 8 7 6 5 4 3 2 Second Edition

First Printing, April 2014
Printed in the United States of America

GIVE ME EVERYTHING

by

Angela Kay Austin

DEDICATION

To strong women everywhere. Survivors.

ACKNOWLEDGEMENTS

If you said to someone you love, "Give me everything." What would that mean to them, or to you? As the idea for this book grew inside of me, I interviewed friends and family to attempt to get an understanding of just what it could mean.

Bearing your heart and soul to anyone is scary. There is the very real possibility that when you do open and offer your heart, the person you want may not respect or reciprocate the gift. And it is a gift.

It's even harder to take that chance when you have fears based on past failures in love and life.

To everyone who's ever been hurt by love, dusted themselves off, and gave it one more try...don't stop loving.

CHAPTER ONE

The solitary inflated tube bounced clumsily down the frenzied river with its four passengers. Cold water from the New River sprayed LaKia Jackson over and over as she dipped her oar into the crystalline water in unison with the others in her raft.

Urgently Terrence shouted, "Nic, LaKia rock...left!"

Terrence and Kendis removed their oars from the water. LaKia and Nichelle dragged their oars in the river and paddled repeatedly until sweat blended with the mist of river water covering their bodies.

"Rock, right!" belted Terrence.

"LaKia watch your right," repeated Kendis.

Concentrating on her left, she had ignored Terrence and Kendis' last call. Her oar collided with a rock, snapping and cracking as it ripped from her hands shattering into smaller pieces. Her fingers quivered from the prickly sensations shooting through them. Her heart leapt from her chest when she saw the rock in front of them. The momentum from her body cast her from the raft.

Kendis caught her around the waist, but his grip slipped.

She fell sideways, rocking the raft, into the water. The vibration inside her helmet as it bounced off the rubber tube rang in her ears.

GIVE ME EVERYTHING

Cold spring water of the New River gorge rushed into her mouth. Gasping for air, she tried to pull herself back into the raft. Her hands were too wet. A sickening wave of terror welled up in her belly. "Nic-, Terrence help."

Frantic, her friends' hands and arms thrashed through the water. They couldn't catch her as they guided the raft around the rocks. Waves of salty water filled her nose and mouth; she sank beneath the water, but her vest buoyed her back to the surface.

She had been trained for this...what was it again? Point your feet downstream, keep your body limp, and protect your head. How do you keep your body limp, when you're scared out of your mind?

Her torso ping-ponged from rock to rock banging her arms and back against every stone in the gorge; slowly consciousness began to drain from her body. Choking from the water in her mouth, she gagged as she slipped beneath the water again. The ragged pieces of her vest, shredded by the gorge's rocks, floated in the water around her.

The arm that pulled her out of the river felt as solid as the rocks beating against her body. For a moment, she thought she wasn't being pulled from the water and that she had drowned. But, then she felt the warm air of summer brush across her cold wet skin; her rescuer's other arm reached down and wrapped around her body to secure his grip. Shivering as she laid on the bottom of the raft, she opened her eyes. Kendis Washington—her enemy, was now her rescuer.

She stirred and awakened as Kendis slid his hands beneath her limp frame. Each shove of her battered body sent a painful shock through her. Fluidly, he scooped her off the rubber floor of the raft and headed toward the dressing tents.

The lantern-lit dirt trail leading to the changing area was covered by indistinguishable shadows and silhouettes to LaKia. She could make out the sounds of small wildlife scurrying about toiling through their nightly rituals, and other guests finishing up their day on the river revving up their car engines to return home. Hickory scented smoke perfumed the air as some rafters prepared for a hamburger, and hot dog medley.

Kendis gingerly navigated the fallen brush and holes dug by man or maybe the local wildlife to bury food or dwell. But, she frowned with the vibration of each step.

She tightened her arms around his neck to control her bounce in his as he carried her to the dressing tent with Nichelle and Terrence in tow. Once inside, she cautiously uncurled her incredibly long legs in search of the cement floor beneath them. She wanted to say something. "Thank...you." Then her words failed her.

"I'm glad you're okay," he responded.

"Me, too. I don't care what you say, you need to learn how to swim," said Terrence.

Terrence and Kendis retreated to the male dressing tent. Nichelle helped her slowly remove her wetsuit. "I was so scared, Ki. I don't know what I would've done if he hadn't saved you." She watched as her friend tucked the tattered suit away into her netted garment bag resting on a bench in the corner. The bear hug Nichelle trapped her in caused her sore muscles to hurt even more, but as her friend's tears fell to her shoulder, she gritted her teeth and hugged her with the last ounces of strength in her body.

Nichelle stepped away and wiped at the tears dangling from her lashes. "But, what a story you have to tell. Gorgeous man scooping you out of the waves and carrying you back to your tent."

Shaking her head rigorously from side to side, she tried to shake the thoughts of Kendis out onto the ground beneath her feet. As much as her body hurt it should have been easy, but she could not stop herself from imagining his arms encircling her again. "No story to tell," she croaked.

13

"Whatever."

With carefully planned movements, she undressed in the tarp tent. "I can't believe I fell in. I can usually lock myself in the raft pretty good." The bruises from her fall prevented her from moving as quickly as her friend.

"Maybe you were nervous."

Cutting Nichelle a what-are-you-talking-about look, she asked, "Nervous about what?"

"Do you remember once when we were at work there was this gorgeous courier that gave you a package, you signed then immediately turned around and tripped over air? He picked you up, and helped you with the box you were carrying." Holding her stomach, Nichelle rested her back against the metal pole in the center of the tent. Her body shook from laughter. "Oh man that still brings tears to my eyes. At least I know you like the way Kendis looks."

"I didn't throw myself out of the raft to get his attention." Secretly, she thought she wouldn't have to work that hard. He struck her as the type of guy that wanted to be noticed and that would take notice of anything in a skirt. "I think I fell out because you and your husband were so busy watching me and Kendis that y'all didn't guide the raft around the big fat rock we hit."

"Well, at least you're okay. "

"Yeah. Thanks."

"But what do you think? Of him? You two going on a date? You know."

LaKia stretched her legs along the wooden bench she sat on, and massaged her bruised thighs as she frowned. "What do I think? We work together."

"Not really." Nichelle slipped on her crisp, dark blue jeans.

"He's gorgeous, but we do work together."

14

"You always look for an excuse."

Annoyed, she responded, "An excuse?"

"Yeah. What happened between you and Derrick doesn't mean you have to shut yourself off from the opportunity to meet someone else—-a good man."

"Every time I tell you I don't want to meet someone, you think it's because of Derrick."

"Well it is."

"No. It's not. What about Tony?"

"Okay. You gave one guy a chance, but it didn't last long and I still don't know what happened with that."

"There's nothing to know...it didn't work out," she snapped.

"I guess not. But this time it was my husband. I told him you were tired of my matchmaking. Sorry girl, but I knew you'd find a reason not to come if you knew only the four of us would be rafting."

"You're right. Remind me to strangle your husband."

"You're a beautiful twenty-eight year old woman whose life is work-work-work."

"I like what I do."

Nichelle stopped tying the lace on her sneakers; stood up, and wagged a finger in her direction. "Good lord, that's not what I mean." She pointed at LaKia's body, and then her hair. "If you put a little effort into the way you dress, your hair, or take a vacation once in a while maybe you'd meet a great guy or at least have a little fun."

"What? Do you want me to walk around dressed like a hooker with a big FOR SALE sign on my forehead?"

"That's not what I mean, and you know it."

"Yeah, yeah, yeah," she muttered.

"Come on out of there ladies. We've changed and we're ready to go." Terrence yelled from outside of the tent.

"We're on our way out," her friend shouted, and she grabbed her ears. Nichelle's yell made her head ache even more. Nichelle threw a hand over her mouth, and only removed it briefly to speak in a whisper. "Oh, sweetie, I'm sorry."

"I'm okay. Don't worry about it. Go ahead. I'll be right behind you."

She had a hard time convincing Nichelle she could finish by herself, but finally she left her alone, and exited the tent laughing as she said, "Terrence leave my girl alone. She's getting dressed." She tugged at the sleeve of his t-shirt in an unsuccessful attempt to pull him away.

Terrence continued to harass her. "Were you ladies talking about me and my expert rafting?" He yelled at Kendis. "Can you believe it, man? I think they're talking about us."

After minutes of coaxing, Nichelle finally managed to drag him away. His laughter faded as he and Nichelle disappeared down the dirt trail toward their cars.

Slowly, LaKia continued to dress.

She shoved her head through the neck of the cotton t-shirt she struggled with. A shadow flickered across a light outside of the tent.

Kendis had paused by the women's changing tent.

Why'd he stop? She thought of how she'd shivered in his arms as their friends guided the raft to the end of the trail. She'd felt fragile in his arms, and for some reason she didn't want him to let her go.

Now as she watched him through the crack in the tent as he watched her, she realized she'd forgotten to re-tie the closures after Nichelle left. The thick canvas doors of the tent had gotten entangled in the debris on the ground, creating a gap.

He had protected her—rescued her, but now...he was like everyone else.

Fifty pounds of dead weight wrapped around her ankles, gluing her feet to the cold concrete floor, impairing each step. Pain coursed through every muscle. Laggardly, she tied each rope.

His eyes scanned her body.

She moved deliberately. The rocks had taken their toll on her leaving her frail and weak. Every time their paths crossed at work they were equals, but now, she was vulnerable. And he took advantage of it.

Her face grew hot as she was assaulted with distant but not faded memories. She squeezed her eyes shut as she remembered how her college sweetheart, Derrick, forced his knee between her legs to keep them from closing. She kneed him in the groin, and dug her cotton candy colored acrylic nails through his t-shirt into his shoulder, he grimaced, but the pain only temporarily deterred him.

Derrick hadn't responded to her pleas. His drunken haze had permitted him pretense to seize her.

Terrence's voice in the distance disturbed her thoughts, and severed their connection. She moved to another position inside of the tent.

Kendis waited for her a few steps up the path.

When she neared him he reached for her hand to guide her up the poorly lit path, appalled by his touch, she snatched her hand away.

"Let me help you. It's dark."

"I've got it."

Cagily plotting a route through the hole-littered path, she tripped on a veiled tree root. Falling, she flung her arms forward, and braced her body for impact. The boulder she banged into sent an undulating pain through her fingertips that mushroomed through her entire body. A whimper escaped her as she pushed herself upright.

Kendis helped her up.

He extended his hand again, this time, she accepted his offer, and they walked up the trail together in silence to join Nichelle and Terrence.

"Kendis can you give my girl a lift back home?" asked Nichelle. "You guys live so close to each other. You're right around the corner on Lottsford Rd."

Screaming inside of her head at Nichelle...she couldn't believe the girl had done it to her again. There was no way to avoid being trapped in his truck for five hours.

"Sure. No problem, if she doesn't mind."

Nichelle turned toward her with pleading eyes. "You guys are only about ten or fifteen minutes apart. I'm almost an hour. I left home at three this morning. It would save me a lot of time. Do you mind?" asked her new ex-best friend.

Through clinched teeth and a tight jaw, she responded, "I don't mind."

Nichelle had a look of mission accomplished on her face as the two couples separated and walked toward their cars. Over her shoulder, she yelled, "Great. Call me when you get home Ki."

Standing at Kendis' truck door, she said, "Thank you for offering to take me home."

"No problem." He opened her door.

Linen scented air wafted around her. Glancing into the backseat she saw nothing. Unsullied polished black leather beckoned her to curl up and nap all of the way home. She grabbed the hand grip; slowly she pulled herself into the SUV.

Kendis nudged her sore torso into the proper position, and snapped her seatbelt across her. "What's your full address?"

"305 Benton Road. Thank you again for driving me home...you didn't have to."

He closed the door, rounded the truck and jumped in.

She watched as he keyed her address into his navigational system.

Settling into his leather bucket seat he responded, "Hey, my Mama would be mad if I didn't help a woman in need."

"And how does she feel about you peering through an open tent," she said sharply.

Flinching, he responded, "I apologize, I didn't mean to stare. I wanted to know if you were okay."

"Whatever, I guess it's the way you handle things."

"What does that mean?"

Crossing her arms across her chest, she penetrated the side of his head with her stare. "You do what you want, when you want."

He was just like Derrick. Eight years had passed, but she thought about it—him—everyday.

"Trust me, if I wanted a woman I wouldn't have to peep in on her." Pressing a button on his steering wheel, he lowered the volume on the radio.

"But you did. What were you trying to see?"

"The door was open. I wanted to make sure you were okay. That's all."

19

"You could've asked. You didn't have to pull up a chair and watch."

"It wasn't like that at all."

"Don't worry about it. I get it. It's who you are. I should've known from work."

A streak of orange tinted sunlight cutting through the tree tops along the highway beamed into his eyes. His leather chair squawked as he shifted his position in the seat. "What...from work?"

"You and your company are taking what you want from small businesses in my mall."

"So, you don't think it's time for development?"

"There's always room for something new, but instead of working with us and the community y'all are going to tear up the environment and close down a hundred small businesses."

"But we'll add thousands of jobs and improve the economy of the city."

"Improve the economy...humph...increase traffic, screw up wetlands, and take jobs out of the community."

"I don't see it that way. Better jobs and more money there's nothing wrong with that."

"There's also nothing wrong with strong communities and families."

Kendis' hands formed fists around the wheel. "Strong families are rare." He turned away from the steering wheel to glance into her eyes. "You sound like an ad for the YMCA."

"Why? Because I care about something more than money?"

"So, you think I don't?"

"I don't really know what you care about...other than naked women." Voyeur.

"I care about more than naked women and money. But, sometimes the things you want don't want you back."

"What does that mean?"

"It means we can't all be like you." He took his eyes off the road; they met her glare. "Super heroes."

Her body stiffened; slim, long fingers bowed into knotted fists. "Huh?" What did he mean by Super hero?

"I've watched you around the council meetings. I see how everyone's always turning to you. I've seen the ads you run. I know how hard you work, but I work hard, too."

Half the reason she worked as hard as she did was because of him. He was more detailed than a lot of the people she came up against. Others always underestimated her company, their influence in the community, and her. "I didn't say you didn't work hard. Your presentations to the council members are always detailed. I have to be ready for any curve ball you might throw at me."

"I believe in what I do. Putting more jobs into predominately black communities is important to me. I think those companies deserve a chance."

"We give new businesses a chance; but, what about the companies already there. Are you willing to throw them out to make room for the new?"

"Why can't there be room for both?"

"We tried that, but your company didn't like that idea."

"No way. I never saw any proposal."

"I was a part of the team that put the proposal together."

"I'll check around. Maybe something got pushed to the side before I joined the team as lead counsel."

"Sure you will." She saw absolutely no reason to trust him.

21

"I will."

Short bursts of conversation speckled their return trip home. Kendis scrolled through the channels of his XM Satellite Radio system. The watery blue block shaped numbers on the dashboard lit up the car interior as they changed.

He turned onto Lottsford Road.

"Right there. That's my house."

Leaning forward in her seat, LaKia examined the house. "Nice."

"Thanks."

"I searched around this neighborhood when I looked for houses last year. You got lucky."

"I know."

He turned onto 202 South. The closer they came to her condo the more regularly the computerized navigational system chimed.

"This is it. Thanks again."

Kendis eased the SUV to a stop.

"No problem." He began to exit the SUV, but his door chime knelled at him. "Wait, I'll get the do..."

She swung the door open. "I've got it. Don't bother."

CHAPTER TWO

LaKia immediately regretted the choice of "Home Sweet Home" for her telephone ringer as it blared in her ear waking her from a restless sleep. Eyes shut tightly, she rocked the receiver in its cradle as she grabbed for it. Lurching up, she opened her eyes to catch it before it fell from the nightstand. Clicking the talk button she said, in a husky voice, "Hello."

"Hi, Good morning!"

Should've known. It was Nichelle and she knew she wanted to talk about Kendis. A groan escaped her.

"How do you feel?"

Nichelle was too bubbly for her first thing in the morning. The Sunday morning sunlight blasted through canary yellow curtains framing the four large picture windows across from her bed. Smashing the phone to her ear and her face into the soft, down pillow, she asked, "What time is it?"

"Wha...a little after 9:00 A.M. So, you're not missing any important body parts are you?"

"Naw, I'm okay, I guess."

"Are you going to make it to church today?"

"I don't think so. I called and left a message telling them I wouldn't be able to teach the self-defense class this week either. I can barely lift my leg. I know I wouldn't be able to show anybody how to do a jab-punch-kick."

"Just checking to see if you needed a ride."

"Thanks."

"So, anyway. What happened last night?"

Rolling over onto her back to get a better grip on the telephone, she used her other hand to pull the fluffy white covers around her neck. Even though it was the middle of the summer, she still had her king-sized bed covered with thick quilts. LaKia muttered, "Nothing. After Kendis dropped me off I was so tired I fell asleep, but I planned on calling you."

A detailed play by play about Peeping Tom Kendis or their strained conversation during the drive back was not how she wanted to begin her Sunday. Nichelle probably wouldn't understand anyway.

"You know, since he works for Eastover that could make things complicated."

Shaking off a shiver that suddenly traveled up and down her spine, she remembered the strength of Kendis' arms when he pulled her from the rapids. His black and maroon wetsuit hugged each muscle as if he were carved from the elastic material. Adonis, Greek God of desire and good looks, drenched in dark chocolate.

She didn't know how long she'd been knocked out, but she knew he held her as she lie on the bottom of the raft because when she woke, she was still in his arms.

Although she had no intent of seeing him again, on the drive back, she noticed the sinewy definition of his arms and chest, normally hidden by made-to-order suits at council meetings. The arms that had held her looked as strong as they had felt wrapped around her.

Instinctively LaKia knew he wouldn't understand she hadn't been intimate with a man in years. Positive he would

24

be like every other man or worse, she promised herself she wouldn't be weak again—especially not with someone she almost worked with daily.

Nichelle's voice rang in her ear. "Maybe, but your jobs don't directly compete. You two don't even work for the same company. He's a lawyer, and you're a marketer."

"I guess, but I couldn't believe it when I saw him. It's a small world. When you told me a friend of Terrence's moved to the area, and you wanted to set me up. I would've never thought it was him."

"I still can't believe that either. Small world."

"Yeah. But you know the way the women at the office chase around behind him. I don't think I want to get involved with any of that. And besides, there's no way he would be able to deal with my no sex clause anyway."

With a sigh of boredom, Nichelle responded, "Every man is not about sex."

"No, every man isn't, but lots of them are trying to get as much as they can get. At least the ones I meet."

"Give it a chance. And maybe you should still give him a chance."

Fluffing the pillows underneath her head, she said, "I'm trying. I don't know if Kendis is a good way to start. Besides, what's his story? Why did you two think we'd be good together anyway?"

"Maybe you should take the time to talk to the man next time, and then you could find out for yourself, but Terrence thought you would be good together. Sorry, I don't really know Kendis' story."

She sat up and rested her back against the supple leather of her headboard; now, she was awake and curious. "If I planned on seeing him again, I would ask. But I don't, so I'm asking you. For your information, I did talk to him...the whole ride home." Kind of.

Nichelle paused before responding, "Yeah, right. But anyway, I don't know the whole story. Terrence only told me a little, but basically there were some issues with his ex-wife."

Being awakened at nine in the morning on a Sunday with her body covered in bruises, LaKia was easily aggravated by Nichelle's evasiveness. "What do you mean some issues with his ex-wife?"

"Like I said, I don't know the whole story, but that's one of the reasons he wanted to leave Ohio. He filed for divorce and left town."

"Divorce. Left town. What was he, some kind of a playboy or something?"

Women at the council building swooned every time he passed by in his tailored suits leaving a lightly, fragranced trail behind. She knew he had more than a few opportunities to be a bit of a playboy, but she never heard any rumors of his conquests around the mall. She was curious to know what the issues were. Knowing men the way she did, he probably deserved it.

"Don't know," Nichelle said, "...but I don't think so. Anyway, don't forget about my party. You're still coming, right?"

"Yeah, I'll be there."

Reading the LCD display on her cell phone, LaKia muted her car radio and tapped the button on her earpiece. "Hey, Mama." Softly, LaKia tapped her brakes; her mother hated her to drive too fast. One of the multi-colored file folders resting on the passenger seat slid to the grey carpeted floor.

"Hi, Baby." The thick, syrupy southern accent of her mother's voice bubbled with love.

"Hey Mama. What have you been up to?"

"Nothing. I haven't heard from you in a while."

"Sorry, I've been so busy with work."

A soft cough came from the other end of the phone. "Are you still working late into the night?"

"Once in a while, but not tonight. I'm on my way to Nichelle's for a house warming or house remodeling party. Or something like that."

"That's good. You need to get out and have a little fun."

Sighing heavily, she said, "Oh, Mama."

"I haven't heard you mention anything about dating anybody in a while. I worry about you being up there all alone."

"I'm okay."

"Baby, I talked to DeWayne the other day, and he told me you were kind of sad."

My baby brother must be punished. "No. We were having our 'if you choke on a peanut conversation'."

"Choke on a peanut conversation?"

"If I choked on a peanut in my basement, who would be there to rescue me? Since I fell into the river, I've been thinking about things like that. That's all."

"What? Why?" Her mother's voice rose to a high pitch before calming back down to its normal soothing tone.

"Because if it wouldn't have been for my friends I could've drowned, and they're not always around. And there's so much I want to do." She knew she shouldn't be unloading this on her mother because it always worried her, but it was on her mind and heart.

27

The other end of the line grew silent for a moment. "You shouldn't think about things like that. You've accomplished a lot."

"I guess," she sighed, "but I want more...not just financial success."

"What?"

"I don't know...lots of things. Look at Nichelle and Terrence...I'm a million miles away from where they are. She is four years younger than me, and she's been married for years, has a new house, and now she and Terrence want to start a family. She has a good job, and he took over his father's business. But me, I bought my condo alone. All of y'all are in Arkansas, and as you always point out...I'm not dating anyone. There's so much I want, Mama."

"Baby, you can always come back home," her mother's voice cracked a little as she finished her sentence.

Sadness overtook LaKia. Headlights of cars in on-coming traffic blurred, morphing into dim white discs eerily illuminating her car.

"Yeah, I know, but what would I do? There are no good jobs for me back home right now. I don't want to slow my career down. It's just sometimes I miss y'all. And sometimes I wish..."

"You wish what?" her mother's voice softened even more.

I wish I was married, and that I'd never left Arkansas.

She struggled to hold back her tears. "Nothing." She sniffed. "Just thinking out loud."

"I thought you were thinking about consulting."

"Yeah, but now wouldn't be a good time."

"Someday soon you will be blessed...like I was with your father."

28

The mention of her father deepened LaKia's melancholy frame of mind. Turning onto Nichelle's narrow tree-lined street, her eyes misted as she pulled into her friends' driveway. A motion detector light perched at the back of the carport lit up the dark night announcing her arrival. Entranced by the fluorescent orange dials on her dashboard, she sat while her car idled. Wistfully, thoughts of a dark prince charming on a white horse flooded her mind, but she was too old for fairy tales.

Her head fell back onto the headrest behind her. "Oh, Mama...if I could be as fortunate as you."

"Don't give up, baby."

Too Late. "Really, I'm okay. You know DeWayne, he likes to think he's Daddy."

"Both of you protect each other like lions," said Lakia's mother through gentle laughter.

"That would make you the Queen Lioness, huh?"

"Of course. Growl." Her mother burst into laughter on the other end of the phone.

Her mother's growl was more like a kitten's purr. She broke into laughter, too. "I don't think that growl will scare anyone." The sadness weighing down her mind and heart, lifted a little. "Mama, I've been sitting out in front of Nichelle's house for a while now. I'll give you a call back later."

"Ok, baby. I love you."

"Love you, too."

Thirty years of working late nights, and early mornings for one of the largest hospitals in Arkansas, put her mother on the trail to Sr. Manager of Payroll at the age of fifty-two. When they were younger, every time LaKia or her brother cried because she was not home, her mother's response was the same, "I have to feed you."

GIVE ME EVERYTHING

She never snitched when her father burned their dinner and took them to Church's Chicken to pig out on fried chicken, fried okra, corn, and soda. When he tangled a comb in her hair that had to be cut out at the hair salon, she didn't say a word. She wore plaits with beads until her hair grew out. He never wanted to worry their mother. He didn't want her to think he couldn't take care of them.

Teary eyes stared at her from her mirror. After re-applying her make-up, she fluffed her hair. Digging into the glove box, she found and blew her nose on a fast food napkin before getting out of the car.

Slowly, enjoying the crisp night air, she strolled up the stone path to Nichelle's front door; she snapped a mental picture of her slice of Americana. Neatly aligned homes with manicured lawns sat noiselessly side by side. The pings of the motor of her car quieting from its forty-five minute drive were her only company.

The grey metal door swung open. Surrounded by light and music, Nichelle's petite, pixie-haired frame hugged her. "'Bout time you got here."

"I had stuff to do."

"Yeah, yeah. Come on in."

Nichelle stepped aside to make room for LaKia to enter.

A hint of anticipation animated her words as she walked through the window-framed doorway. "So, who all is coming to this function?"

"Just a few friends," said Nichelle with a mischievous grin.

Over the weeks, she hadn't been able to get Kendis off her mind. With the help of Nichelle, she thought about him every day. Still, she'd made it clear nothing would happen between the two of them, and that was the best thing. However, she had to admit it was hard to stop the barrage of memories that attacked all of her senses as she watched him at work. It'd been a long time since she'd thought of a man in this way.

Scoping out the crowd, she noticed some of the changes they'd done to the living room: new carpet, paint, and furniture. The white walls were now yellow, the wood floors had been replaced by thick long-napped brown carpet, and their old floral print furniture was replaced with leather couches and chairs studded with brass tacks along the seams. The television sank into a built-in alcove above the fireplace, and DVDs filled curvy metal and wooden afro-centric holders.

But she didn't see him. "Who did you invite?"

"You could just ask if Kendis is here." Grinning, Nichelle continued, "He's in the basement. By the way isn't that the dress you call your watch out there now dress?"

"Hmm, this old thing." LaKia thought she'd seen his black Chevy Tahoe parked outside, but there were a lot of cars and everybody drove SUVs except her.

"Yeah, that old thing," Nichelle replied, snapping one of the straps on LaKia's green sundress.

"You don't know everything about me...do you?" She gave her friend a mock frown. Come to think of it, Nichelle didn't know everything, but she knew a lot. LaKia hadn't consciously planned it, but it took her much longer than usual to get dressed. Nothing she tried on seemed good enough until she put on her green sundress. She had asked her reflection, "Would Kendis like it?" But, she kept that to herself.

"Hey, girl, I forgot to tell you Tony is here."

She bit back a groan. She'd dated Tony—tall, motorcycle-riding gym rat—about a year earlier. It hadn't ended well. Since then she hadn't dated anyone.

Although Terrence didn't ride motorcycles anymore, he and Tony had belonged to the same motorcycle club. When Nichelle met Tony, she couldn't wait to hook her up with him.

GIVE ME EVERYTHING

According to Nichelle, he was searching for the perfect wife. Turns out, it wasn't her.

Whenever they talked, he always called her beautiful. It made her feel special. Feeling special to someone was all she ever wanted, but she found out she wasn't his most special someone.

They would have great conversations about everything, when he remembered to call. They would make plans: to take trips, to go to dinner, or the movies, but he never followed through. Angry, she would fall asleep by the phone...waking up the next morning with a crook in her neck as a reminder.

Back then, sex and food, were top priorities for Tony, but because of his key-toting ex-girlfriend sex between the two of them never happened.

"Let's go say, hi," said Nichelle as she turned and walked toward the basement with LaKia following closely behind.

"Can I have a drink first?" she yelled over the music.

"Sure, we'll stop in the kitchen, and grab a couple of beers for the guys, too."

LaKia felt her sandals sink into the plush new carpet as she and Nichelle threaded their way through the crowd of people to the kitchen.

Gliding down the stairs in single file, LaKia followed Nichelle into the basement. Until Kendis saw her, he hadn't realized he'd wanted to see her.

"Hey guys, we thought you might need a little something to drink." Nichelle sat her tray on a table that doubled as a chessboard. She handed a beer to Terrence.

"Thanks, Babe."

Kendis couldn't muzzle his smile when he saw LaKia. The green sundress she wore hugged her lean body. With feline-like grace she walked toward him carrying a couple of bottles.

Bewitched, he glanced over every inch of her. Lime green never looked so damn good. Without trying, his mind jumped back in time to their rafting trip. Aside from the bruises left by the rocks, her skin had looked flawless. Scanning every visible inch of her body, now, he couldn't find a hint of imperfection.

Her lips were full, and the lip-gloss she wore made them look ripe and inviting. The bounce of her breasts played against his stolen memories of her leggy physique. The thought of tasting her mouth and feeling the friction of her skin against his excited him. He was thankful to be standing by the pool table because he could feel his manhood rise. After their last conversation, he knew that if she saw him with a hard on she would think he was the biggest freak around.

"Kendis, do you want a drink?"

He didn't know how many times she'd said his name before he heard her. "Sure," he replied as he reached for the emerald colored bottle. "Sorry about that. Thanks. I could use a drink." Maybe the beer would cool his ass off and down. Swallowing the cold, brown liquid, he sank into the shadow of the pool table hoping LaKia couldn't see his body's reaction to hers.

He kept his eye on the brother he'd met earlier, Tony, as he inspected LaKia with a familiar eye and an alligator smile. The man's bold desire for her annoyed the hell out of him.

Tony winked at LaKia as she handed him a drink. "LaKia do you still play?"

"I was never any good at pool." She walked toward a leather chair in the corner of the newly renovated basement.

Nichelle and Terrence had done a great job renovating, LaKia thought as she took it all in. They had everything: dart board, pool table, video games, and of course his center piece--a projection screen TV. It was no longer a basement, but a game room.

Tony's broad smile didn't dim, "Yeah, but it was fun watching you play."

"LaKia, why don't we play? It'll be them against us, but we'll need a third," Nichelle piped up.

The split second the words rolled off Nichelle's tongue, her cousin, Tina, appeared at the bottom of the stairs. Tina had a degree in dance and music that she paid for by working as an exotic dancer. LaKia didn't know any woman who could move her body the way Tina did simply when walking.

She took a long, searching look at Kendis wanting to see his reaction to Tina...was she his type?

She watched as Nichelle asked Tina to join them, and introduced her to Kendis and Tony. Quickly glancing from Tony to Kendis, she noticed the stark difference in their reactions as their eyes traced Tina's snaky trek through the room. Tony's cartoonish reaction—wide eyes and open mouth—was expected, but Kendis' calmness wasn't.

"Okay, let's get this game started." Terrence said as he handed Tina a pool stick. "Ladies first. I'm sure the men won't mind."

With a pert little wiggle to her walk Tina followed Terrence around the table; she came to a dead stop in front of Kendis. The distance between them disappeared. Kendis put a hand on her hip, and took a step back.

"Would you mind showing me how to hold the stick?" she asked in an octave usually only audible to small animals.

LaKia should've known Tina would make a beeline to Kendis. Now, I'll find out what makes him tick.

"I'm no expert. Maybe one of your teammates can help you out." He pointed at Terrence. "Or him." The other man smiled and waved off his suggestion. Traitor.

"No," she purred. "...I think you would be a much better teacher."

She removed his hand from her hip, and turned to lean over the table. With a quick glance over her shoulder at him, he leaned his body close to hers. Her hands vanished beneath his. LaKia felt flushed; her stomach knotted up as he touched Tina.

The black skirt Tina wore rode up her thigh as she bent over the table allowing Kendis' denim covered thigh to rub against hers. His height gave him a perfect bird's eye view of her melon-breasted physique; her low-cut blouse offered no resistance.

With fluid motion, his right arm slowly moved into position along hers to grab the end of her pool stick. They slid the pool stick through their fingers to the beat of the music. Finally, the stick burst through their fingertips and cracked against the balls.

"Go girl, that's how to play pool. We're stripes. Hey Ki it's on you," Nichelle announced.

Circling the table to determine the best shot, LaKia could not figure out why she was agitated by Kendis' interaction with Tina. If she'd wanted him she could have had him on the rafting trip, during the ride back to her house, or at his house. Or, any occasion at work. "Yeah, yeah I'm analyzing the table."

"Look out guys, her eyes look serious." Kendis smiled at her with affection. Phony.

"But that dress says she's not," said Tony.

LaKia cut her eyes at Tony, and then she banked the nine ball into the right corner pocket.

"You two made her mad." Terrence accused, his gaze bouncing between Tony and Kendis. "Leave her alone before we lose this game."

After sinking her ball, LaKia walked back to the cheering women's section. In her excitement, she hugged Tina before she plopped into one of the buttery leather chairs.

Strutting over to the men's section, Nichelle threw her arms around Terrence's neck and pecked him on the cheek. "Well gentlemen it looks like the women came to play pool. What about you?"

"And what do you want as a reward, babe?" Terrence stroked Nichelle's face with the back of his hand.

Tony threw a chalk cube at the doting couple from the other side of the room. "Can you two be in the same room and not touch each other?"

"Don't be jealous," Terrence laughed, lobbing the cube back in his friend's direction.

"Jealous? LaKia and I have plans of our own." Doing his version of Nichelle's strut, he stopped next to LaKia, threw his arm across her shoulders, and said, "Don't we, babe?" He looked down at her with a slight little grin.

Tony's large, muscled arm weighed her shoulders down. Why not say yes? She didn't know what he had planned, but she didn't think it would hurt for Kendis to know other men found her attractive, too.

"Sure." It was the only thing she could manage to say.

"Really?" Tony couldn't hide the surprise in his voice. Continuing with their lie, he said, "We thought we would go to LaKia's favorite little coffee shop, The Chocolate Drop. Any of you guys want to join us?"

Walking toward the table to take her shot, Nichelle looked at her with a disapproving eye as she blurted out, "LaKia, you didn't mention anything to me."

"It's on the way home. And we haven't seen each other in such a long time. We thought we could catch up."

Nichelle missed her shot.

"Oh, babe, how'd you miss that? You couldn't stand to see your husband lose, huh? Kendis, start us off, man."

"Alright. Four ball, top left pocket."

In a voice dripping with sex, Tina purred, "Kendis, do you need any help with your grip?"

Kendis chuckled in response. He couldn't help it. Over the past year, he'd had a lot of women like Tina. There was a time when she was exactly the type of woman he wanted. He thought. Now that he'd met LaKia he wasn't so sure anymore. Keeping things professional at work became more difficult each day, and their friends didn't help any. The Tinas of the world didn't ask for much, which was perfect because he didn't think he had anything left to give them, but women like LaKia wanted everything. He'd given that before, and it hadn't worked either.

"I got it." He lined up his shot, and leaned over to strike.

Tina dragged her hand up and down his back; he missed his shot.

"Man, you missed. Your concentration must have been affected by your partner," chided Tony.

"I guess." His concentration was off, but not because of Tina. Shit. Why should he care? LaKia and the muscle head dude, Tony, had plans for the night.

37

After he took his shot, LaKia left the basement. Silky, green fabric flitted around her ankles as she disappeared at the top of the stairs.

Impulsively, he followed her.

Rummaging through the mini wine refrigerator, her body formed a perfect ninety-degree angle. His pelvis found her rear before he had time to stop.

Wine bottles clanged against each other.

Startled, LaKia swung around. "What are you doing? You like sneaking around don't you?"

"I'm sorry, I didn't see you."

"Okay, whatever." She spun back towards the small, stainless steel wine refrigerator.

Now what? She can't stand you. "So, are you the designated bartender?"

He shook his empty bottle from side to side. "Since you brought me the first one, I thought you might refresh it, too."

"Depends." She quipped with her back to him as she searched for something in the mini refrigerator, she asked, "Are you a good tipper?"

Reaching into his pocket, Kendis pulled out his wallet and removed a twenty-dollar bill. He handed it and his empty bottle to her. "Another barkeep."

Taking the money from his hand, she stuffed it into her bra. "Thanks." Then she searched through the chilled bottles swimming in cold melting ice for another Heineken. Before she could hand him his beer, she had two other people waiting for refills at the marble-topped island in the center of the eat-in kitchen.

Kendis sprang up from his seat. He scavenged the white painted cupboards for an empty bowl and placed it on the counter. "Tip your bartenders."

It was the first thing he'd done that made her laugh. He hadn't seen her laugh before. Mysteriously, she only had one dimple, and her round eyes virtually disappeared. Her laugh was warm and contagious. He and everyone in the kitchen laughed, too. Twenty minutes later they had served a bunch of girly drinks Kendis wasn't very familiar with: Frozen Italian Bellinis, Ice Cream Sandwiches, and Mojitos while they re-enacted scenes from Tom Cruise's Cocktail.

When the crowd dwindled away, LaKia and Kendis cleared away the mess they'd made. He'd broken two glasses, and had promised Terrence, when he came searching for them, he'd replace them with his tip money.

With her hands covered in dish soap, she blew at strands of hair that had fallen into her face. Kendis brushed the auburn streaked curls away from her eyes, pinning them behind her ears. The slightest touch of her skin against his fingertips drew an instant reaction from his body. He stepped away and dropped his hand to his side.

She fixed her eyes on his. "Thanks."

"No problem."

Standing next to her as she washed the silver martini shaker, Kendis struggled with controlling his thoughts and desires. Each move she made accentuated her long legs, apple bottom, and bosom. As he passed behind her to put away some of the dishes he'd dried, he was overcome by her scent—soft and floral.

He wanted to hold her, kiss her, and nibble on those petite little ears holding back untamable red curls. Bury his face in her neck and inhale.

Placing the last dish back in its original place, Kendis picked up the overflowing tip jar and handed it to her with a grin. "You can treat me to dinner with this."

Flashing him a smile that was a bit less friendly, she pushed the jar into his chest adding the twenty dollars he'd given her earlier. "You can keep it."

Why subject yourself to this? Twenty minutes ago he couldn't be scraped off Tina with a spatula. Why should she be the runner-up? He probably only wanted sex. Her or Tina. Now, she had no doubt he didn't care where it came from.

Maybe he thought sleeping with her would help him with his job. He wouldn't have to work as hard proving the value of his project because she would make it easy for him, but he was wrong.

The pool game had continued in their absence. It was the last shot of the game, and Tina studied the table hunting for a shot. She glanced up, saw Kendis returning and quickly picked up where she'd left off. The entire night she'd hovered around him, and this moment wasn't any different. Tina caught him before his foot hit the bottom step.

"Come on Kendis, I've got another shot, and I suck without you."

"Sorry I think I'm finished for the night." He headed towards the corner of the room where he'd sat earlier.

She sauntered back to the table, and with a single stroke, the eight ball sped toward the left front pocket. Apparently, she didn't need his help after all.

Placing his pool stick back into its grip on the wall, Tony said, "That's game." Jingling his keys his pocket, he asked, "You ready?"

She held Tony's gaze. "Sure. Let's go." She turned towards Nichelle. "Thanks for the invite. It's been great. I'll call you tomorrow."

"Thanks for everything." Tony squeezed her shoulder as he winked at Nichelle.

Sweeping her eyes across the room, she walked up the stairs trying to avoid any sort of exchange with Kendis. "See everybody next time."

Rummaging through her purse for some lip-gloss, LaKia watched through her car window as Tony strolled across the parking lot toward the entrance of The Chocolate Drop.

She re-touched her gloss before hopping out of her car, and rushing to catch him. The quaint little coffee shop was one of her favorite lounge spots, but she didn't come much anymore because of the crappy light in the parking lot.

Her shoes clicked at a rapid pace against the asphalt. She hurried across the dimly lit lot. When she caught up to him, he asked, "Most people wouldn't know this place was here. How'd you find it?"

"I was a regular at the gym next door. I didn't like the gym—too many people ogling you instead of working out. But I always came here afterwards to relax before heading home."

Tony opened the door letting it close behind him, but LaKia caught it with her sandal clad foot. The aroma of chocolate, caramel, and cinnamon surrounded her. She watched him flag down a waitress. He led her toward an empty table flanked by two over-stuffed blue and red chairs. Once seated, she ordered a latte with heavy foam and cinnamon. Tony ordered black coffee.

"I can't believe you agreed to come."

GIVE ME EVERYTHING

LaKia rocked in her chair to the soft R&B playing through the Muzak system. "You know I love this place. It always smells so good. The coffee, pastries..." She closed her eyes, and dragged in a long slow breath.

Tony eyes crawled across all of her before he said anything. "You still look so beautiful. And that dress." He licked his lips, catching his bottom lip in his teeth, making a slow sucking noise as he let it go.

LaKia patted her stomach as she pictured her dusty treadmill in the corner of her basement covered with laundry. A year ago, he would've told her she needed to do some crunches. But she accepted the compliment with a smile and a nod.

"So, tell me LaKia what have I missed in the last year?"

Adding sugar to her latte, she responded, "Nothing much, really."

"You know I think about you all the time. What went wrong with us? I really cared a lot about you."

Slightly irritated by Tony's question, she said, "Tony, you know what went wrong."

"So, you never forgave me."

God knows she wanted to forgive him, but for all of the wrong reasons: his ripped abs, perfect smile, or that sexy little goatee which felt incredible against her skin. But she didn't love him and he definitely never loved her.

When she didn't answer right away he asked again. "You never forgave me?"

She bit her bottom lip while she carefully considered her words. "I don't know...maybe."

"So, what then? Why are we here?"

The look on his face made her uneasy. He was staring at her so intensely, that she wanted to get up and walk away. "Because you asked, and we're adults."

"Are we adult enough to go to dinner, too?"

"Dinner?"

"If dinner doesn't work for you, then how about lunch sometime next week?"

As much as she hated to admit it, Nichelle was right again, she was still scared of being hurt by another man. But Kendis didn't scare her. In fact, she liked capturing his attention, and she didn't like sharing it with Tina.

Tony didn't scare her either. Falling in love with him would never happen.

CHAPTER THREE

Faint rumbles from Kendis' stomach reminded him of the coffee he drank for lunch. Tired as hell and hungry, he pulled into his garage a little too close to an oversized ceiling to floor wood cabinet.

Initially, the overwhelming support for the project by the local community fueled their efforts. Eastover and Brady—his law firm—believed the town mayor and council members would fully support a new 2.5 million square foot mall loaded with big box retailers. Filings of their conceptual drawings, and proposals were picked up for local news stories, but because of one gorgeous determined woman, their progress slowed to a damn crawl. The citizens of the town had begun to fear they would lose their small town vibe. The possibility of too much growth too fast had become their biggest enemy.

As he turned the key in the lock to the side door of his home, he heard the phone ring. The shrill sound bounced off high beamed ceiling through empty rooms, and rattled along wrought iron accented windows and doorways. Although he'd lived in the house for a few months, he hadn't taken the time to shop for furniture. The week he moved into the house he purchased a grill for the patio. Later, he replaced the tile floors with hardwood, as a result, the house was a cave, every sound echoed.

His footsteps smacked against the floor as he sprinted through the laundry room to grab the phone hanging on the stucco wall of the kitchen. Only two people had his number in

Maryland. Terrence and Carl FitzSimmons—his boss. Nobody else. And he liked it that way. He checked his watch again. Terrence never called this late. He could hear his voice asking the caller to leave a message; he picked up the receiver before the person could respond to his recorded request.

"Hello."

"Hi, Kendis. It's Tina."

"Tina." Damn "How did you…"

"I hope you don't mind, but I asked Nichelle for your number." Before Kendis could say what he thought, she continued, "Did you know Nichelle was my cousin?"

No.

"I wanted to call and thank you for the pool lessons the other night."

Next time he would remember to check the caller ID. "No problem."

"Would you like to go to dinner?"

"Thanks, but I don't have a lot of free time." He didn't want to hurt her feelings, but he wasn't interested. Why in the hell did Terrence and Nichelle give her his number anyway?

"Kendis are you turning me down? It's only right that you let me thank you properly."

Thank him properly. He knew Tina didn't get turned down often, but he wasn't looking for another Tina in his life, right now, and he didn't feel like talking.

Looking down, he realized he had sprinted all of the way to the kitchen with his briefcase in his hand. Leaning around the corner to check out the side door, he saw he'd left it wide open. He didn't have anything to steal, but he didn't need to invite them in either.

With the cordless telephone to his ear, he walked back through the laundry room dropping the briefcase to the floor in the hallway as he did. Twisting the knob of the deadbolt, he said, "When?"

"Friday. O.K.?"

"That's good for me. What time should I pick you up?" "Nine o'clock?"

Damn. That meant he'd be dropping her off late. He knew he would need a hell of an excuse to get out of this woman's house at night. Why did she have to be Nichelle's cousin? If she wasn't this conversation would've been over.

"What about something a little earlier. How about eight?"

Quickly, she answered, "That's good. Plus it'll be Friday night. You need a little time to play, right?"

Since his divorce a year ago, he'd played enough for a hundred men. It all got old...fast. He didn't know what he wanted, or why he was confused.

"True, Tina, but right now, I'm working on a tough project."

"O.K., eight at my place."

"No problem, I'll get directions from you next week. Bye."

"Bye."

Cousins. They were two extremely different types of women. Replaying the party in his head, he was sure nobody had said anything about being related to Tina. Didn't matter. He texted Terrence. Better have a good ass reason for giving Tina my number.

LaKia felt light-headed; she grabbed the closest cart from the corral and pushed the squeaky wheeled basket into the grocery store. Farm fresh peaches and plums filled the air with the scent of their nectar. She sampled garden-fresh pineapple and a new chunky veggie dip the grey haired demonstrator handed her.

Everyone in her spinning class appeared to be in much better shape than her. She was wiped out from a single thirty minute class. As she walked, pain needled her calves and butt. It had been awhile since she'd been to the gym, but she didn't think it would hurt like it did.

With all the pressure at work—advertising, lobbying against the new development—she barely had time for anything, but since she'd met Kendis and had her latte with Tony she'd decided to renew her gym membership.

At work, she preferred dark knee-length suits: black, royal blue or maybe dark green accented with bright blouses. She didn't want to hide her body, but she didn't want to give the wrong impression. But if a man, Kendis in particular, wanted a woman like Tina with her short skirts and tight shirts how could she compete?

Her body wasn't shabby. During her weekly visits to her stores, she had more than her share of GQ wannabe store managers, district managers, or shoppers showering her with compliments.

She had never dated anyone at work, or connected to her job in any way.

But, somewhere between bouncing off the rocks of the New River, Nichelle's party, and her date with Tony she decided to make some changes. At twenty-eight, she grew more tired every day of coming home to any empty house and her cat.

A male voice calling her name disturbed her thoughts. She didn't have to look long or search hard to figure out who called her. Kendis Washington walked straight toward her down the center of the aisle. Hemmed in by rows of juice she saw no escape.

What was he doing here? The long basketball shorts he wore covered most of his thigh, but not his legs; every muscle in them flexed as he came closer. The blue cotton sweatshirt stretched around his broad shoulders barely contained his large biceps. Maybe he'd played basketball in the neighborhood somewhere. He looked delicious. She looked a hot mess, but she hadn't planned to stay in the store long or bump into anyone she knew. As she inspected her cart she realized she didn't have a thing in it. She'd been walking through the grocery store aimlessly pushing an empty cart.

She hadn't seen him since the housewarming party, but the smile on his face convinced her of his excitement to see her.

"Hi, LaKia."

"Hi."

Pointing into her empty cart as he stood in front of her, he said, "Can't make up your mind?"

White tile covered with a colorful vinyl ad for apple juice stared at her through the gaps of the metal cart.

"No, I know what I'm looking for. I thought I would take a look for something different for a new recipe I saw last night."

Kendis stared at her like he'd caught her in a lie. What did he know?

"Yeah, what recipe? I love to cook, if it's any good, maybe I'll try it, too."

"Maple glazed Salmon with red potatoes. The recipe requires apple juice." It wasn't a total lie. Last month, she'd seen the recipe in one of her cookbooks and wanted to try it. The recipe needed apple juice. Perfect reason for wandering around in the juice aisle.

"Sounds good. Any specific type of apple juice? Maybe I can help you find it." He scanned the shelves. "I cook a little something once in a while."

She tugged at the bottom of her oversized t-shirt trying to get it to cover more of her butt and hips. "Thanks, but I got it."

"What? You don't believe me?" Kendis grinned warmly.

"I believe you. You look like you work out and take care of your body. You're probably a pretty good cook." Truthfully, she didn't want him too close. At least not looking like she did. Her face felt hot as she pictured herself through his eyes. Old, sweat-stained gray jogging pants and an extra-large t-shirt courtesy of the Red Cross hung from her body. Her curly hair, crazy and wild, sticking out of her ponytail clip.

Waiting to shower at home was a big mistake. She could smell the dried sweat stench of her own body.

Next time she would shower and change at the gym and this wouldn't happen. She didn't want him to help her find anything. She wanted him to go away.

"It was good bumping into you." She began to back away.

"Wait a minute," he grabbed her cart.

"What?"

With a cautious look on his face, he asked, "Would you be interested in going out with me next week?"

LaKia could swear she saw little beads of sweat forming on his forehead.

"Might be fun." She always had business cards on her. She took one out of her bag and flipped it over. "This is my home number. Call me with the details."

She preferred to let him do the calling. She'd chased after and ran from enough men. At least this way, she could gauge his interest. A man like Kendis would not waste his time chasing a woman if he wasn't attracted.

"Is the middle of the week a good time to give you a call?"

"Sure." Scanning the aisle, LaKia discovered the apple juice behind her. Backing the cart up slowly, she leaned to the side to pick it up, and asked, "Do you remember how to get to my place?"

Smiling, he said, "I saved it in my navigational system."

He saved it. Trembling fingers held the apple juice she'd picked up; she tossed it into her cart. "Okay."

"Maybe Saturday."

"Saturday would be good."

"I'll give you a call around Wednesday."

Kendis turned and walked away, but he stopped for a second at the end of the aisle and glanced back. When he saw her watching him, he waved.

LaKia stood still and watched him disappear around the corner. She headed in the opposite direction, no need for him to see the sweat stains covering her butt.

Why was he in this grocery store? He didn't have a cart, groceries...nothing. Nichelle.

Dropping her bags onto her small kitchen counter she called Nichelle before she unpacked her groceries. As soon as she heard her voice, she asked, "Did you send Kendis to the grocery store?"

"Busted. Lakia figured it out," she yelled out to Terrence. It wasn't me, it was my husband."

Giggling at Terrence's attempts to set her up, she asked, "Do you know what I looked like at the store?"

"No, tell me."

"Humph." She put away her groceries as she described her appearance to Nichelle. By the time she finished, Nichelle's laughter had turned into snorting.

Privately, LaKia wished she could be as content and happy as her friends. Maybe she could find a man, marry, and have a family...eventually. As it stood, something always went wrong. What if things could be different with Kendis?

Speaking in a loud voice that Terrence was sure to hear. Nichelle said, "I told him you'd be mad."

LaKia grunted as she stretched to put away a can of stewed tomatoes in a cabinet above the sink. "Tell him he's officially off of my Christmas gift list."

With those two working as a team, she'd never be able to put Kendis behind her. No man had affected her mind and body like Kendis in a long time. Whenever he took over her thoughts, she could feel the blood rush through her body, and all rational judgment escaped her. She couldn't stop her mind from wondering what it would be like to be close to him: to feel him wrapped around her, holding her, kissing her...making love to her. Making love. She hadn't been intimate with anyone in years, and the last time she tried it was a fiasco. But more frequently, as she watched him argue his case, she had to stop herself from fantasizing about his touch.

"How did Kendis react when he saw you? Did he run?"

Cheerfully, she said, "No, he asked me out."

"Now, you know you've got it regardless of whether you're wearing Rocawear or funky wear," said Nichelle between giggles.

She visualized Nichelle pinching her nose with two fingers, and she laughed, too. "Ha ha you're so funny." As her giggles quieted, she asked, "Did you ever ask your husband the rest of the story on Kendis?"

"Yeah, and he told me to mind my own business."

"Wha..."

"No, he said you should ask Kendis. He doesn't know the details. They lost contact for a few years, and then he called him to say he was moving here."

Raking her fingers though her hair she wondered why he hadn't told Terrence.

Her other line clicked. She folded the last of her grocery bags into the green, plastic, recycle bin. "Hey, that's my other line, I'll call you back." Pressing the flash button, she switched to the other line. "Hello."

"Hey, Beautiful."

Tony.

She had completely forgotten he promised to call.

"Hi, Tony. What's up?"

"What's up? Did you forget about me?"

"It hasn't been that long." A week.

"I guess not," he said softly. "So, when are we going to do this?"

"Do what?"

"Do what? Catch a movie, dinner, or something."

A movie would be good because they wouldn't have to talk. But she'd had a week to think about it, and she'd changed her mind.

Because Tina damn near gave Kendis a full-body massage in front of her, she had agreed to coffee the night of the party. She could admit that to herself. But, she would never admit it to Nichelle. She knew the woman would have her picking out a wedding dress within the hour, and married by midnight.

"B. Smith's in D.C. Thursday for lunch around one?"

She did love their food, but it might be a bit too romantic for her and Tony. She would like someplace more casual like Taco Bell. "I love their food."

"Great, I'll meet you there."

"Wait a minute, I meant..."

"What?"

Tony's voice softened. She didn't want to hurt his feelings. He was a nice guy, but he wasn't the guy for her. "That's fine."

"Can't wait to see you."

CHAPTER FOUR

Thirty minutes, and Tina still hadn't made her way downstairs. Kendis drove to the end of the crescent shaped lot and tapped the button for his hazard lights. A sixty-something portly light-skinned black man wearing a dark blue uniform clicked his flashlight against the car window.

"Move the car, sir."

Slowly, he lowered the window.

"I'm just waiting on someone to come down."

"You can't sit here, if we have to keep warning you we'll call the cops."

Damn. I've been driving around forever, and only been parked for a minute. He fought the urge to curse the man out. It wasn't him that had him waiting. He leaned out the window slightly to glance up and down the street. "There's no parking on the street."

"That's not my problem, sir."

"Okay, okay." He didn't want to be there anyway.

Shadowing a couple walking hand-in-hand, Kendis waited until they pulled away from the curb—a block away from Tina's building, and then stomped back toward her apartments.

His eyes followed his finger as he searched the list of names. 3-0-5-#.

Tina's voice burst through the speaker. "Hello."

"It's Kendis."

She buzzed him into the building. No excuses or apologies.

Music hummed through the walls of the elevator; the doors opened, and Kendis stepped into a house party. The thinly carpeted floor throbbed underneath his feet from the baseline in the music; groaning, he realized the music came from Tina's apartment. The shiny brass doorknocker tapped out its own beat before he touched it. Why didn't her neighbors complain?

He banged on the door to compete against the music, thinking about the ass kicking he'd promised Terrence earlier in the week for giving his number to Tina. But, to his surprise, Terrence and Nichelle were clueless. After Nichelle grilled Tina, she confessed to getting Kendis' number off their caller I.D. Bold ass woman...bold and a liar. What in the hell am I doing here?

The thought of canceling the date flooded him with relief, but Terrence had bribed him with a chance meeting with LaKia. He chuckled to himself as he remembered the shocked expression on her face when she saw him. Her beautiful eyes rounded and widened as her body stiffened. She probably thought he was a stalker or something.

Strands of fly away hair flared out all over her head. Sweat stained clothes told him she'd been to the gym. Rosy cheeked, bright-eyed, and glistening; she was beautiful.

He hadn't been able to take his eyes off of her.

Hell, since the rafting trip he couldn't stop thinking about her. She was different. Nothing like Kim.

His ex-wife would never walk out of the house with one strand of hair out of place—not even to the end of the driveway to pick up the damn paper. High maintenance and the center of attention twenty-four/seven was the only way to describe Kim.

Onerously incensed air choked Kendis; he coughed to catch his breath. Amused, he stared at the source. The robe Tina had draped around herself didn't cover much. Copious amounts of silky pink fabric flowed loosely over her thickset body.

Smiling sheepishly, she asked, "Would you like a drink?"

Walking past her, Kendis stepped inside of her apartment. "No, I can wait until we get to the restaurant." He hoped refusing a drink might be a way to speed her up.

He marked off a mental checklist: music, half-naked, and liquor. Run man, run.

She trailed through the apartment behind him. "Should we call and push back our reservation? It was for nine o'clock, right? We've only got about thirty minutes."

"Thirty minutes is plenty of time. We should be fine."

He couldn't figure out what she needed to do other than get dressed. The tightly drawn ponytail that swung from the back of her head bounced around on her shoulders as she neared. Thinly arched eyebrows and deep burgundy colored lips hid her natural attributes, but she looked exactly the way she did when he met her.

Tina dropped her hand from her robe as she slinked toward Kendis exposing her black and tan leopard print bra and floss-like G-string. "If we can't make it, we could always stay here and order in."

He slid to the opposite end of the cracked, black-leather couch. "We should have plenty of time, but maybe I'll take you up on your offer another time."

He wanted to send her to her bedroom like he would a child, so she could get dressed and they could leave. But, he didn't. Every day since they'd first spoken on the phone, in some cases several times, she called to confirm that nothing had changed. It annoyed the hell out of him. Now that he was there, he couldn't get her out of the damn apartment.

"On second thought, do you have any cognac? I could pour myself a drink while you finish dressing."

Excitement showed on her face. She grabbed his hand, and dragged him across the room to the small brass trimmed glass bar jammed in a corner of the living room between the couch and the wall of the kitchen.

He slid his hand out of hers. "Would you like me to make you a drink while you dress?"

She rubbed her cheek along his arm. Chestnut colored make-up stained his powder blue shirt.

"Same over ice."

Kendis poured the two drinks—hers on the rocks his neat. Raising his glass to his mouth, he threw his head back. His glass emptied. She rattled her drink around in her glass for a moment, and then she copied his action.

"Now, let me see what you have planned to make every man's head turn tonight."

Tina's mouth broke into a huge smile before she turned and jiggled through the apartment disappearing down the hallway. "Wait until you see what I've got for you," she squealed over her shoulder.

Kendis knew she would want to dazzle him.

After what felt like hours, but must have only been about fifteen minutes at most, she reappeared in the living room dressed to impress. All black. Short, tight, and black. Deep burgundy lipstick. Caramel cheeks were bruised with brick red blush, and her eyes vanished behind black tarantula lashes.

Glowing with a sense of job-well done, she asked, "Kendis, what do you think?"

What could he say? "You look the same as you did when I met you."

The college-aged valet parking cars outside of the restaurant whistled his approval of Tina's outfit. Horny testosterone-filled waiters and busboys hovered around their candle-lit table like dogs in heat. Kendis chuckled to himself as he watched Tina soak it all in. It didn't bother him. If one of them had the balls to step up and ask her for her number, he would concede and leave. But, he rarely received a challenge from anyone.

Black scuff marks streaked the mahogany floor as he pushed his chair away from the small table; he excused himself and searched out the men's room.

Standing in the back of the restaurant he watched. Tina secreted away several small pieces of paper into her purse. She craved the attention of men—lots of men. He made his way through the maze of patrons to their window table.

After he and Kim separated he longed for the attention of a lot of women. They helped him forget her, but nothing made him forget his daughter. Kim didn't want him. Never trust your friend with your woman. But, tons of other women did. And, as often as possible, he gave them what they wanted as long as it didn't get complicated.

Staring quizzically at him, Tina asked, "Is there something wrong with your steak?"

Kendis had dissected his Carne al Paso into small pieces while his mind wandered through his past. "It's good. Just cutting it up."

"So, what does a new lawyer in town do in his spare time?"

"Not much, I work a lot."

"No time to play."

The twinkle in her eye as she said "play" reminded him of a look he'd seen many times before from several women. He repeated, "Not much."

"So, you know my cousin through Terrence?"

"Yeah."

Suspending a forkful of cheese filled tortilla in mid-air, she studied his face as if seeing it for the first time. "I don't remember you from the wedding."

"I was married." Kendis knew it wouldn't take much more of an explanation. He was sure she had searched out every eligible bachelor at the wedding; he'd fallen below the radar. Although he knew that probably wouldn't stop her every time.

As if nodding her head in agreement with his silent thoughts, she said, "Oh."

Cheese mixed with pico de gallo dribbled from the corner of her mouth. A tongue the length of Gene Simmons' slithered across her lips to capture the small pieces of tomato and cheese before they dripped onto the table.

Forty-five minutes later, Kendis sat in front of Tina's apartment complex.

Slowly, her hand slid her skirt higher up her thigh. "Kendis, why can't you come up for a drink?"

"Thank you for the offer, but I have a heavy schedule in the morning. I don't think I'll be good company tonight."

"I promise," she leaned in closer. He could smell the gin on her breath from her drinks. "...it will be worth your time."

For too long, his truck idled; his hazards blinked an S.O.S. to the flashlight police.

The same elderly guard approached the car. "Sir, please move your car."

Content, Kendis said, "No problem." He put his truck in drive. To Tina he said, "Maybe, another time."

Persistent as hell, he didn't think she'd give up, but she did. A few months ago he would've taken her up on her offer, but not tonight.

The weekend was almost over, but he had one last perfect day to kick back with his grill and a beer. Steam bellowing from the grill blinded Kendis, briefly, as he flipped some burgers in his backyard—one of his favorite features of the house. It reminded him of Tennessee. Instead of Bratwurst and burgers, he'd probably be grilling some ribs and chicken. His mom would whip up some potato salad, and his dad would chill the beer. The yard would be filled with his younger cousins playing ball. His aunts and uncles would pull out the card tables. Spades. Dominoes. Maybe even Uno. Mosquitoes would send the party indoors, but they wouldn't stop it.

A backyard jam-packed with children, and a house heaping with love and laughter is something he thought he had figured out.

LaKia could share his backyard. Man where did that come from?

He plated some burgers on buns with the works: mustard, lettuce, tomato, and onion he didn't think she'd eat from his menu because her body looked perfect. But, maybe they could sit back and watch the golf match.

It'd been a long time since he'd simply sat beside a woman on a couch and relaxed. Now, he didn't even have a couch to sit on—one day he would furnish this place. Usually if he spent any kind of time with a woman they ended up in bed. If she could handle it—not get clingy, he would go back for seconds on a different day, but if they called too much or needed too much he'd move on.

After loading his plate with a healthy serving of hamburgers and bratwurst, he popped open a beer and headed toward the stairs leading down to his basement.

He'd splurged on a home entertainment system, which included the biggest television he could have mounted on his wall with a kick ass sound system. He wouldn't need all of that for a golf match, but during basketball and football seasons it would be perfect.

He set his Corona on the folding table beside his favorite leather chair, the only furniture aside from an oversized ottoman and the television, and he kicked his legs up on the stool in front of him, one of the burgers fell against his stomach. "Damn." He caught it before it hit the floor, and he laid back to enjoy his golf match.

The doorbell rang.

Annoyed by the Sunday afternoon disturbance, Kendis climbed the stairs to the living room. He stood paralyzed as he stared at the uninvited guests at his door.

"Daddy!"

His body jerked from the impact of the small child that clamped onto his leg.

She stretched her arms up toward the sky waiting for him to pick her up. A beautiful little 18-month old. Two long braids hanging to her shoulders, big round eyes, and a large bright crooked smile.

She didn't look a damn thing like him. Unable to resist her request, he bent over to scoop her into his arms. Standing behind her silently watching everything was his ex-wife, Kim.

Why were they at his front door...and with luggage? He'd moved out of the state because he didn't want to worry about her popping up at his door. But here she stood in front of him with their baby.

Swooping Keisha up into the air, he hugged her until she giggled out the word Daddy. He kissed her on her forehead as he instructed her to go inside and play.

"Am I invited inside, too?" asked Kim as she stood on the porch peering around him to scan his home.

Keisha vanished out of sight.

Blocking her entry into the house, he held his position. "Why in the hell are you here, Kim?"

Pressing her hand to his shoulder, she pushed in an effort to pass. "Keisha wanted to come and visit you."

"Keisha." Rage punctuated his words. He moved aside to let her enter before his neighbors took notice. "We agreed you would explain everything to her." He controlled the urge to throw her back out of the house and slam the door behind her.

"She wanted to see her daddy."

"Then you should've taken her to see him. It sure as hell isn't me."

"You are."

"No, I'm not. What the fuck do you want, Kim?"

Slowly walking through the house towards the backyard, she inspected each room. "Grilling? Are you expecting company?"

Standing his ground, refusing to be anything other than cursory in his tone, he responded, "Is that any of your business?"

She tossed her hair over her shoulder and called her daughter's name, "Keisha."

Her daughter's small feet made a steady soft clapping sound as she ran up the stairs in response to her mother's voice. She lunged into her mother's arms, with a piece of bratwurst dangling from her mouth.

Clutching Keisha in her arms, like a shield, she cautiously closed the space between them. "Haven't you missed us?"

"Missed you..." Kendis took the little girl from Kim's arms. He hugged her and whispered, "Daddy loves you." Tickling her belly, he put her back on the ground. "Go back downstairs, sweetie."

Laughing, she ran towards the stairs and disappeared back into the basement.

"Kim, you and I had an agreement. You signed the papers. We're over."

Anger raced through his body, but he still noticed her beauty. Diva. Keisha was almost two, but you would never know Kim had had a baby. After Keisha's birth, she went to the gym everyday trying to lose the weight, and her body showed it.

They'd met at a club in Cleveland while he was still in the Marine Corp reserves. Every man in the club wanted her, but he was the lucky one to take her home. They dated for six months before they married. He hadn't planned on getting married, but he did because Kim convinced him it was the best way to make sure she would be taken care of if he were ever hurt while away for the reserves. "You never know what might happen," she'd said.

His family never warmed up to Kim, especially his mother. Constantly, his mother asked, "Why doesn't she wear her wedding ring on the proper hand?" For some reason, Kim wore it on the right finger, but the wrong hand.

Kim closed the gap between them as he pondered the past. They stood in the middle of his empty living room surrounded by nothing.

She kissed him. He grabbed her by the arms and stared into her eyes. This woman destroyed his life. And here she was in front of him, wanting him back. Why?

"Do you still love me?"

"Are you cra...Lov..."

She kissed him again. He didn't push her away. Not because he liked it, but because he didn't. Kim never had to work hard to get a reaction from him: the sound of her voice or the flick of her hair would set his body on fire. But now, his body wasn't responding to her. He didn't crave her touch. Releasing her, he stepped out of her reach.

"We thought we would stay for a while."

"No."

"Why not? You have plenty of room."

"I don't care why you're in town or how long you stay, but it won't be here. I'll drop you at a hotel after Keisha finishes eating.

"Whatever." Turning to walk away from him, she vanished down the stairs to join her daughter.

Because he didn't have any furniture, Kendis sat on the carpeted floor in his basement looking at Kim in his chair as she dozed. As he watched her head roll from side to side, he reviewed the timeline of their relationship. Married and divorced before 30.

He hadn't known a lot of people in Ohio, but that was okay, because he only needed Kim. She was all he thought he wanted.

But, he was not all she needed or wanted. She needed: the biggest house on the block with the best car parked in front of it, and unlimited shopping. Dollar after dollar seeped from his pocket and bank account.

And when it came to family, the only reason she agreed to start working on a family was because her girlfriends were having babies. But, he knew she didn't want to mess up her body. Or, stop her partying.

After Keisha's birth, he asked her about going back to work. Her response, "The women in my family believe when a woman has a child that is her job."

His mother worked forty years for the Post Office and his father worked forty-five years as a School Bus Driver. Telling his parents she didn't plan to go back to work after the baby was a mistake. Aside from saying hello if she answered the phone when they called, they barely said a word to her. The news of his divorce being final spread through the family like the news of his first-born child.

Hearing the changing voices from the television as Kendis surfed through the stations must have disturbed Kim's nap.

"What time is it?" she asked, rubbing her eyes as she stretched.

Since it was Sunday, he didn't have on a wristwatch. He read the digital time display on the television channel guide. "A little after midnight."

Taking a look at his empty plate, she asked, "What do you have to eat?"

"Check the kitchen. In case you're wondering, I carried Keisha upstairs to the guestroom after she fell asleep."

She scanned the room, and sunk back into the leather chair.

He rolled his half empty beer bottle back and forth between the palms of his hands. "So, tell me why you're really here?"

Smiling down at him from her position in his chair, she asked, "What? You don't want to see your family?"

His hands tightened around the bottle as he glared at her. "I don't have a family."

Quickly raising her voice in anger, she shrieked, "We might not be married anymore, but we were a family."

What in the hell gave her the nerve to say they were a family? It felt like ten thousand volts shot through his body as he stared at her without the rose tinted goggles.

Selfish ass woman. Keisha probably didn't matter to her either.

Steven Phillips'—young, black auto dealership millionaire—baby would set her up for life a lot better than having his baby. Something must have gone wrong with her plan, but who gave a damn.

Slamming his beer bottle to the floor, he roared back, "Until you fucked it up." The beer spilled onto his leg. He jumped from the coldness against his bare skin. "What? Steve didn't make enough money for you or you weren't good enough for his family?" Steve came from an old black money family in Cleveland. Steve had warned him against marrying Kim. So, how could he betray him? He knew Steve's family would never accept her or their child.

Kim let her temper flare back. Flailing her arms, she paused briefly to point a finger in his face. "Money? I got my own money."

He rose from his seated position on the floor; she drew back her finger and retreated into the cushions of the leather chair. He shook some of the beer from the right leg of his khaki shorts and he walked toward the stairs to the kitchen for some paper towels. Gazing down at her, he said, "No, you've got my money and maybe some of Steve's. What, it's not enough for you?"

Silently, she followed him.

Grabbing his hands as he pulled paper towels off the roll, Kim erased the space between their bodies and gazed into his eyes. Tilting her head, robotically she placed cold dry kisses on his neck. The feel of her cheek brushing along his chin left him apathetic. Warm and wet her tongue tried to slip through his tense lips.

Again, he grabbed her. This time, his anger won. "What the fuck are you doing? Stop with this shit."

She pressed him into the stove; the oven handle poked him in his ass. Her hand invaded his pants massaging, angrily.

"What is wrong with you? You show up at my door, and what? I'm supposed to feel like I won something."

"We're back. We can be a family again. Keisha and I can move down here."

"No."

"I hear you're doing really well down here. You've got enough space. Why not?"

"You hear I'm doing well?" He pushed her away. "From who?"

"Friends and family."

He adjusted his clothes, and turned to walk away. She lifted the blue jean skirt she wore, and waited. She never wore underwear.

Leaning against the sink, she lifted her skirt higher, but the sight of her body did nothing to him. She no longer held any power over him, except Keisha. He loved his daughter. A current of sadness flowed through his soul.

Kim shouted after him, "Keisha wants to go to the amusement park."

He looked back to see her still leaning against the sink examining herself in the reflection of a spoon.

"I'm dropping both of you at a hotel when she wakes. I'll take her to the park, but I don't care what happens after that."

She lowered the spoon to glare at him. A smirk replaced her deadpan stare.

CHAPTER FIVE

Exhausted, LaKia slouched over the meeting room table. The windowless grey room filled with easels and whiteboards dulled her senses. Glancing at the clock on the wall, she sighed as she realized she'd been in the meeting for more than two hours. Since Eastover's plans had been presented to the city council, her days had been filled with things to do for one planning committee after another.

Endless strings of meetings, press, phone calls, and impromptu visits from mall merchants requesting personal updates drained her. She may not have had much of a life, but, lately, she wasn't in control of it.

Her date with Tony would be her get out of jail free card. She needed it.

Taking another look at the clock, she realized she was about to be late. She'd thought twice about keeping the date with Tony because revisiting the past wasn't something she'd set out to do. But, forgetting about Kendis Washington and an excuse from these never-ending meetings were two good reasons for keeping it.

Apologetically, she rose from her seat at the horseshoe shaped conference table. Coughs and rustling papers signaled the committee members' disapproval. With her armful of folders, she kept walking.

The drive time from the council building to the restaurant wasn't much, but lunchtime traffic morphed her short drive into an hour commute.

GIVE ME EVERYTHING

Tony waited.

"Hi, Tony. I hope I didn't keep you waiting too long. The commute sucked."

"It's okay. I know how you are about time. You didn't call to cancel, so I knew you'd be here."

LaKia reached for her own chair, pulled it out and sat down; she read over the familiar menu to see if anything had changed. She hadn't been to B. Smith's for a while. But, at one time she had been a regular—once or twice a week.

Pub tables covered with burgundy and white tablecloths combined with subdued candlelight and instrumental jazz calmed her after a long day of complaints and cries.

Her mind floated back to breezy summer night dinners on the brick patio. The jazzy beats of the band controlled the night's tempo. Before she'd know it, the restaurant would be shutting down around her. The only problem with the evenings, her dinners for one created an atmosphere of pity. Waiters, waitresses, bus boys, and bartenders felt sorry for her: hovering while she ate, or striking up casual conversation.

They meant well, but she stopped going.

"May, I take your order?" As the waiter took LaKia's order he smiled. Tony noticed. LaKia smiled back, and asked for a Chardonnay and a grilled chicken Caesar salad. Tony ordered a Vodka Tonic and a burger with fries.

"Ki, what have you been doing since I saw you last? How's work been lately?"

"Work is good. Eastover is still a threat, but we're preparing for the next round." She did not want to discuss work, but she didn't want to be rude either. "What about you? How's the personal training business going?"

"It's not. I don't do it anymore. I'm back in school, part-time at nights, to finish my degree in IT."

Bartender, barber, real estate investor, personal trainer and now computers.

"Congratulations on your career change. Computers are a good industry to be a part of right now."

"Yeah, I think so. But, why haven't I heard anything from you?"

"Huh?" She knew he would ask, but she didn't think it would come before her meal. Tony always liked to play it cool, but not this time.

She would've liked something in front of her to divert her attention and his. "Work has been crazy."

He reached across the table rippling the table cloth as he took her hands into his. "You've had a little spare time. At The Chocolate Drop you told me you couldn't forgive me. What do I have to do to change that?"

"No, really, I've been drained. Long meetings and appointments." She ignored his last question.

Her hands thumped the table when he released them. Annoyed, he asked, "Do you want to spend time with me or what?"

Why would she after the way their last date ended?

Tony could easily win over anyone with his big-hearted smile and easy-going laugh. Aside from his hints about her need to get into Greek Goddess-like shape, she knew she couldn't forgive him. How could she?

"Tony, what can I say? I can't believe I'm here, but I am. You had me in your bed and then..."

"Yeah, I know. I should have been straight with you and let you know I had a woman."

Pausing, her water glass at her lips, she said, "You think!" She sipped, and returned her glass to its proper place next to her wine glass.

GIVE ME EVERYTHING

Elbows planted firmly into the tabletop, the taut fingers of Tony's hands emphasized each word as he spoke.

"When I realized she was coming over, I tried to get you out."

"Yeah, by covering it all up with another lie. Calling your friends over to play cards and asking me to participate until my ride showed up."

Defensively he replied, "You didn't tell me your girl dropped you off. I thought you'd parked in the lot and walked to the front door."

In a rising voice, she asked, "Did it really matter? Why did you disrespect me by putting me in that position? Why did you disrespect your girlfriend...yourself?"

Looking across the table into his eyes, she knew her words wounded him. But he asked.

"When your phone rang I was sprawled across your bed stripped down to nothing but my fricking Victoria's Secret. I didn't know what the hell was happening. Then, your friends arrived with snacks and cards. You didn't even have the guts to tell me what was going on. What was your friend's name...David? He told me."

"I know."

Nausea crawled through her whole body as she remembered that night. By the time Nichelle showed up, LaKia sat on the couch beside Tony's girlfriend playing spades.

The vibration of her phone in her purse was like hearing an angel's voice. She was free. Running for the front door, she'd held back her tears long enough to walk out of his house.

The next morning, he called to apologize. She cursed him out, hung up the phone, and hadn't seen him or spoken to him again until the night of Nichelle's party.

"Right now, I can't promise anything to you. I'm trying to do some things at work. Depending on what happens with Eastover, I may or may not have a job." If Eastover couldn't be stopped, she would definitely have to find another job, but she already had offers from other companies, and her own company had promised her another position.

He slid his chair closer to hers, and placed one hand on her thigh. "But maybe. Maybe we could get together again?"

She slumped back into her chair. "I don't know. I've got a lot on my plate right now anyway."

His hand stopped moving, and he sat back. "I understand about the job thing. Are you looking for jobs in the area or somewhere else?" He waited.

She sipped from her wine. "I guess a little bit of both. I've been here a long time. It might be time to go back home."

"Well, I guess I might have to pack my bags." He laughed. "Maybe I can convince you to make enough room for one more."

Before LaKia could respond the waiter returned. She didn't think she'd ever been more excited to see food. At least she would get a moment to get her thoughts together. After the waiter finished setting out their plates she glanced up and noticed Tony quietly waited on a response.

Something LaKia couldn't pin down flitted across Tony's face.

His gaze drifted away. Out of curiosity, LaKia tracked his stare; turning to glance behind her, she saw what had diverted his attention. He sat in a zombie-like trance as a woman in the distance approached their table. The midriff shirt she wore displayed her washboard abs—they made her pat her soft mid-section. Tony's posture became stone like, but LaKia watched as the rhythm of his breathing synchronized to the sway of the woman's hips.

The nameless woman stopped beside Tony undisturbed by LaKia's presence. "Hi, Tony."

LaKia recognized her. She should since she played spades with her.

Tony responded, "Sharon."

"What are you doing here?" she asked.

Gesturing toward LaKia with a nod of his head, he said, "Having lunch with an old friend."

A friend? Two seconds ago, he wanted to know why LaKia hadn't called him. Why had she lost contact? Now, she was just a friend. He will never change.

Tony and their uninvited guest ignored LaKia as they carried on their own private conversation.

LaKia interrupted them. "Excuse me, Tony; are you going to introduce me?"

She wasn't going to sit at the table and be ignored by him or his girlfriend again. The woman scanned LaKia from head to toe before she shook her hand. A vague flicker of recognition crossed her face. After mumbling something inaudible to LaKia into Tony's ear, she turned and walked toward the restaurant's bar.

Straightening her posture, LaKia rested her hands in her lap. "So, Tony is that who you're transitioning from?"

With a blank stare on his face, he said, "Huh."

"Tony, we're friends. Nothing more. We tried. But maybe it wouldn't be worth trying again. This type of situation with you keeps popping up."

"It's not like tha..."

Unable to hold back an awkward laugh, she said, "Sure it is. How'd she know we were here?"

"I don't know."

"Tony, you don't have to play dumb with me, it's not worth it."

In a low, sad voice, he said, "So, what now then?"

"We finish lunch and that's it."

"That's it?"

Feeling a lot more relaxed now that she didn't have to pretend anymore, LaKia reached for her fork, and moved her plate closer to her.

Tony shifted around in his seat. He looked overwrought. But why? What could he possibly expect from her? After someone—his girlfriend—tracked them down, did he think she would get back with him? She had no desire to go down that road again.

"Sure. Why would you want to start something with me, when it's obvious you haven't ended what you're doing with her?"

"There's nothing with her."

"Tony, haven't we been here before?" asked LaKia with annoyance in her voice.

"I never meant to hurt you." She crossed her legs and swung her foot to the beat of the music. Her words slowed to match the rhythm.

"But you did. You made me feel like I was nothing more than a piece of ass."

She could tell from the way he avoided eye contact with her and fiddled with his food that he didn't know how to respond.

"I wanted you."

"But you had no right to have me. For eight or nine months you lied to me. Never telling me you had a girlfriend. You should have let me make the decision to be a whore."

"I never thought of you like that."

"No, then what do you call a woman screwing a man in another woman's bed?" She said with a mouthful of lettuce.

Sourness in his voice, he said, "It was my house, my bed."

"But she had the key. And it wasn't her you asked to keep quiet or pawned off as a date for your friend."

Tony sipped his vodka. "I just..."

"You just what...wanted to sleep with me, right?"

Bowing his head, he continued to shuffle his food around on his plate making little piles.

"Is that all you want now, Tony?"

The table was quiet while LaKia waited for a response; the restaurant quieted, a soft hum replaced the jazz saxophonist in the background. He didn't say anything, LaKia kept talking, "And here we are, now, you still have a woman...the same woman chasing you down...putting me in another awkward situation."

"LaKia, I never wanted to hurt you. I've thought about that night a lot. Every time I thought about calling you, I couldn't. I thought you hated me, but then Nichelle invited me to the party and you accepted my invitation for coffee, I thought maybe...we could try again."

Try again. The only thing she wanted to do that night at Nichelle's was get out of there because she did not want to see Kendis with Tina. If she were totally honest, she did not want to see Kendis with anyone.

For once, she knew he was being completely honest. They hadn't seen each other in quite a while, and until the night of the party Tony hadn't seen or spoken to Terrence since the Holiday party last year. Since Nichelle and Terrence had decided to start thinking about a family, they cut back on a lot of things: Terrence sold his bike, Nichelle stopped shopping every weekend, they stopped eating out as regularly, and they put the savings into their baby fund. With the bike gone, Tony and Terrence didn't see each other much.

"Nichelle invited you because I never told her. I told her you were pressing me about sex and I was tired of it."

Stunned, Tony asked, "Why?"

LaKia couldn't really understand his question. He knew why. What woman wants to tell her best girlfriend she was in the bed of a man she believed cared for her only to find out moments later he had a girlfriend.

"Because I was tired of telling her about all of the crazy men in my life. And you, you were...*are*... a friend of her husband's. I wanted you to be different."

As the words fell from her mouth, LaKia knew that somewhere inside she wanted Kendis to be different, too. But what if he ended up being like Tony a good friend to Terrence, but not good for her?

"But I wasn't," said Tony softly.

"No, you weren't. And you're right. I haven't been able to let it go."

"So, now what?"

"Like I said, we don't do anything, but agree to be as we are."

They ate in silence. Unburdened, she thought maybe she could take it further and be as straight forward with Kendis.

With sunken shoulders, Tony said, "I wanted to try again."

"Why, Tony? Even now, you've got the same woman chasing you down."

"I want to share my life with someone."

"Why me?"

79

"Why not?"

"That's not good enough, Tony. I don't want to be any man's last resort. I want to be his first choice."

The shock in his voice as he responded told LaKia what she wanted to know. "You are my choice."

"I'm your choice for now, but what about later, when that woman that just walked out calls? Will I be your choice then?"

"I need you back in my life."

"Why?"

"I need to settle down."

Settle. He considered her to be a runner-up. What?

With sarcasm in her voice, she said, "Settle down, huh."

"You're the kind of woman a man can settle down with. You don't ask for anything. Simple."

She took a moment to sip from her wine glass. Slowly, she was losing calm. "Sounds like you're looking for something easy. I'm not a consolation prize. I haven't been sitting around waiting for you to come back to me. For you to make me the lucky one."

He slapped his knife and fork to the table. "I didn't say that. You're taking everything I'm saying wrong."

LaKia scanned the room to see if anyone noticed the noise Tony made with his silverware. No one did. But if the heat in her cheeks was any hotter it would set the hair resting on her shoulders on fire.

"How should I take it? You're basically telling me you think I'm some simple, easy to please woman...by the way you never once said you loved me."

He choked out the word, "Love."

Feeling a rush of hunger, LaKia finished the food on her plate as she said, "Yeah, do you love me? Why should I change everything in my world for you?"

"Because we could start over again."

"Tony, how do I start over again with you when we have such a weird history?"

"I don't know."

"That's what I'm saying. I don't want the man in my life to be unsure. I don't want women hunting him down. I don't want him to ignore me when I'm sitting at the table across from him, or lie to me to get me into his bed."

Tony slumped down in his chair. Wide-eyed, he stared at LaKia as if she'd just broken his heart.

Guilt consumed her. Why? She was perfectly within her rights to tell him how she felt. He caused it. She had been so embarrassed by the way he'd treated her. Why should she feel guilty? He didn't. She felt like saying to him the same thing he had said to her then, "I'm sorry," but she didn't.

"Tony, do you love her?"

He didn't answer.

"Tony, do you love her?"

Slowly, he began to speak in a low voice. "I...don't know. Maybe. Yes."

Calmly she leaned back in her chair. "I thought so. So, why are you here with me?"

"I don't know."

"Yes, you do. What did she whisper into your ear?"

He folded his napkin into a tight burgundy knot. "Nothing."

"Come on Tony, keep it real. What did she say?"

Pointing over his shoulder at the bar, he said, "She said she'd wait for me in the bar."

"So, go."

With his mouth hanging open he repeated her. "Go."

"And you'd better hurry before she leaves."

He tripped over his words as he reached for his wallet. "La-, La-, LaKia, I'm sorry."

"Bye, Tony."

She eyeballed the money on the table—the first tab they didn't split. After finishing her desert, she left the restaurant, and drove through the bumper-to-bumper traffic back to her office.

Hopefully, her date with Kendis would be better.

CHAPTER SIX

Jacketed and sweater-clad Washingtonians darted back and forth to and from the Red Line subway station across a deserted Connecticut Avenue in front of Kendis' firm's building. The cold glass of the modest circular window pressed against his forehead as he mulled over his life.

He wondered, as he spied on the people below, who would go home to their wives or husbands, their children, or to eat alone in front of the television. Steak, beer, and a game...any game would've been his routine on a Saturday, but Kim kept showing up at his place, and he hid out at work.

The clock on top of the bank across the street flashed two o'clock in red before it flipped to show the temperature. He'd been working for hours revising a proposal he needed to re-submit to the City Council.

LaKia had run a hell of an ad campaign reminding the community of how the small mall had supported the community...providing jobs, and contributing to the city's economy for half a century. She'd done a good job of educating them about possible ecological disruption, loss of small mom and pop businesses, and traffic congestion.

Eastover may have picked the wrong location.

Just the thought of her made him smile. Until now, Kim was the only woman that had ever commanded his attention—held all the cards. This thing with LaKia differed because without knowing it, she called the shots. He had no idea what to do next with her.

GIVE ME EVERYTHING

After Kim he hadn't wanted someone special. So, for a while he had fun with a lot of different women. And it wasn't hard, a man simply needed a halfway decent job, a place of his own, and a nice car and he was in with eighty percent of the women he dated. Without making any promises, women would hand it over on a silver platter. But, now, he didn't want them or it from them, anymore.

LaKia didn't fall for the bull. Under normal circumstances, he would've had most women in bed by now. Flash a smile, take them to dinner at one of the white table cloth restaurants in Georgetown, and he could sit back and wait for them to come to him, but not this time.

His sneakers squeaked against the pine-stained floor as he walked across the imposing office, which had been designed to his specs. Built-in floor to ceiling bookshelves, circular windows on three walls, and sparsely furnished. Aside from the sizeable oak desk and conference table there was little furniture.

He dragged his leather chair away from the desk, sat and called Terrence to get his opinion on his plans for the evening. It wasn't the most macho thing he could do, but he wanted the night to be fun and memorable.

When he heard Terrence's voice on the line he spoke, "Terrence, what's up?"

He could hear the television full blast in the background. Nichelle's laughter swelled up over Terrence's voice.

"Not much, man."

"You know what LaKia likes, right?"

"What she likes as far as what? You might need to talk to Nichelle."

"I was thinking about Jillian's. What do you think?"

"She loves that place. Stay away from any of the racing games. She'll eat you up."

"We'll see. Thanks, man. I hope your girl is cool."

"Just don't break her heart, man." Terrence laughed. "Or, Nichelle will put a hit on you."

As Kendis hung up the phone a lump formed in his throat, he didn't plan to break anyone's heart. He was only trying to protect his own.

LaKia couldn't believe she wasn't ready, yet. She hated being late for anything. She ran from room to room to find her misplaced bracelet. Her mother had given it to her and she rarely ever took it off. She'd been on the phone with Nichelle preparing for her date with Kendis, discussing everything in her closet when she lost it.

The bracelet belonged to her Father, and before him, it belonged to his mother. When he passed away, LaKia's mother gave her the simple piece of gold jewelry. But before her mother passed it on, she'd added a charm—a gold replica of Tweety—the nickname her father had given her because of her eyes.

Throughout her childhood, she and her father were inseparable. She loved her mother, and she and her brother talked almost every day, but she cried for her father often. She couldn't count the number of times, she'd accidentally picked up the telephone to call and tell him about her day.

The night Derrick raped her she prayed for her father's protection as she barricaded herself into her dorm room afraid that Derrick would use his key to enter while she slept.

Date rape is what the counselor called it. The female counselor said, "Date rape is hard to prove. Lots of people get hurt. Reputations get ruined." LaKia walked out of the counselor's office, and never spoke of it again—except with Nichelle.

GIVE ME EVERYTHING

Leaving Arkansas for college in Washington, D.C. had been her way of getting away from the pain in Arkansas. But she found pain in D.C., too.

Maybe, it was time she stopped running.

She would not be able to go on this date without her bracelet. Not without her father's protection.

Nichelle wanted her to be sexy, but she didn't want to be just sexy, she wasn't sure of where they were going, and Kendis had instructed her to dress for fun. The weatherman had said the temperature would be 75o F, but summer only had a few more weeks, and the night air nipped at your bare skin. So, she decided on dark blue jeans, beaded sandals, and a flirty fitted blouse. At least, she would be prepared in case their date went late. It might not be the sexy Nichelle wanted: heels and a short skirt, but she thought it was fun.

The sound of the doorbell tore her away from her search. As she stood in her entryway, she gawked at the gorgeous man in front of her. He hugged her, and kissed her cheek. The feel of his lips against her skin and his arm around her body sparked a forgotten desire within her.

He wore a white cotton shirt and jeans. She welcomed him into her condo. As he walked past her, her eyes skimmed his body—his jeans fit his butt perfectly, it looked firm and hard. The denim fabric rested against his thighs which looked thick and solid. It had been a while since she'd felt excited about a date or a man. What was happening to her? "Kendis, would you like anything before we leave?"

"No, I'm good."

Motioning for Kendis to sit on the couch, her shoes clicked against the wood floor as she headed toward the stairs. "Okay, I lost my bracelet. Can you give me a second to find it?"

"Sure, do you need help?"

Pausing midway up the stairs, she looked down at him sunken into the pillows of her overstuffed sofa. She searched his face for a sign of some sort of ulterior motive, but she didn't think one existed. And the bracelet was too important. "You don't mind?"

"No."

Heading up the stairs toward her bedroom with Kendis only a few steps behind, she felt a subtle tingling course up and down her spine. "It should be in my bedroom somewhere."

Hanging on the walls of the stairwell were photographs of Malcolm and Martin mingled in with pictures of her and her friends and family. Kendis studied each one.

Hesitating at LaKia's bedroom door before he entered, he felt like a kid. As if he had never been in a woman's bedroom.

The cinnamon tinted orange colored walls were adorned with African-American paintings and boxed art. The canopy bed, covered with a yellow down comforter and bright buttercup and tangerine hued pillows invited him to lay in it. The glass vanity in the corner by the closet, filled with perfume bottles, would break if she added another. A mixture of strawberries, pears, and apples scented the air. A few stray pieces of clothing lying on her bed were the only things out of place.

Swallowing to get rid of the lump in his throat, he asked, "Where do you want me to begin looking?"

Walking to the closet, she said, "The only place I stood was here in the closet."

Kendis could see a faint hint of color creep into LaKia's apple cheeks. He smiled at the knowledge of understanding LaKia had spent time preparing for their date.

He realized if she tried on different outfits, she must have tried to match shoes up to them like any woman. "Did you try on different shoes?"

LaKia's mouth formed a slow curvy smile and her eyes widened. "Shoes?"

"Yeah, maybe it fell into one of them."

As LaKia reached into her closet to grab a pair of red shoes, Kendis noticed a stuffed Tweety—it looked old and loved.

"Yeah, I tried on these." Shaking the shoes upside down over her bed the gold bracelet fell onto her comforter. "Thank you."

Without stopping, she kissed him.

Without thinking, he kissed her. His hands explored her body, while his tongue searched for hers. He found it. She tasted like strawberries.

The silk blouse she wore made her caramel skin feel sensuous and silky in his arms. As her hair brushed across his face he could smell her shampoo—light and soft. He pulled her in tighter to his body trying to make their bodies become one, and covered her bottom lip with his mouth.

His body responded to the desire he had for her. He could feel his manhood come alive. Her body felt unresisting in his arms. A shockwave went through his body because suddenly he heard Terrence's words, "Don't break her heart." Regretfully, he pulled himself away from her. Gazing into her eyes, he could see her confusion. He had lost control, but why didn't she stop him?

Putting his right hand to his face, he massaged his temple with his thumb, he said, "We should head out if we want to get there."

With a dazed and confused look on her face, she said, "Head out."

Did she want him to continue? It felt like she did, but where would it end? In her bed? Turning his head away from the bed calling his name, he knew he needed to get out of there. He wouldn't be able to resist much longer if she kept looking at him as if she wanted him. She looked just as hungry as he felt for what could happen. But that couldn't be, up until now, she hadn't shown any real interest. When he asked her out, she didn't even ask him for his number. Most women would have been throwing their number at him, and not just one: home, work, cell, everything.

Finally, Kendis responded, "Yeah."

Confused, LaKia still couldn't figure out what had happened in her bedroom when they pulled into the mall parking lot. She thought he'd wanted to kiss her, but then he pulled away. What? Was he no longer interested or what? Suddenly, she felt stupid for thinking about it anyway. She had put herself in a dangerous position. It would've taken nothing for him to throw her into her bed, Derrick would have, so would Tony—but he didn't. Instead he backed away from her. LaKia couldn't figure out what she wanted. Why was all of this getting so complicated? Why even think about it anymore?

Walking through the parking lot towards Jillian's, one of her favorite hang-out spots with her friends, a brisk wind reconfirmed her choice of outfit.

Kendis puzzled her. Why did he run away from her? Why'd she let him run? The next thought made her smile. What if...what if Kendis stopped because he cared for her?

As they walked inside, she asked, "Can you sing?"

Slowly, he shook his head from side to side, "No, singing isn't my thing."

"You know they have karaoke here?"

"Yeah. Are you challenging me or are we talking about a duet?"

"Duet? What type of music do you like?" LaKia had to raise her voice to be heard above the music and noise of the crowd in the room as they maneuvered through the game room hunting for the bar.

"R&B, Country, Jazz, a little bit of everything."

"Alright, how about something old school?"

"If you can handle old school, I've got the perfect song."

"What?"

Kendis left her at a cozy little table for two, and headed towards the DJ booth.

When he returned, she asked anxiously, "What song?"

"Dennis Edwards and Siedah Garrett's 'Don't Look Any Further'."

Raising an eyebrow in disbelief, LaKia said, "For real?"

"Yeah, why?"

"That's such a romantic song."

Pulling a chair up next to LaKia, he said, "You don't think I know how to be romantic."

"I'm not saying that...I'm just saying...that's such a romantic song."

Beaming, Kendis asked, "Can you handle it?"

Before LaKia could say anything, the roaming spotlight stopped on their table. The DJ announced their names, "LaKia and Kendis."

LaKia responded to Kendis' question as she stood and walked toward the stage. "I can. What about you?"

Kendis didn't respond.

The words written in big white letters came up on the screen. They disappeared as Kendis sang. While they sung, he wondered if she could be the person in the song. Studying LaKia as she danced around the small wooden stage to the music he knew he wanted the words she sang to be for him. So, he sang back. The man and woman in that song had found what they wanted, and didn't want the other person to search for anyone else. The words meant more than she knew to him.

She harmonized with his voice.

Disappointment filled Kendis when the song ended. Grabbing LaKia's hand, they handed their mics back to the DJ. He guided her back to their table. After showcasing their talent with two more songs, they headed out to the game room where LaKia beat him on every game they played.

When they arrived at LaKia's condo at the end of the night, she did not want to get out. If she got out of the car, the night would be over. Not including the fiasco with Tony, it had been a long time since she'd gone out on a real date.

They both sat quietly in front of her home.

An uneasy flutter made her stomach queasy; her face felt flushed. She swore if the streetlights were brighter he would see the red in her cheeks. Kendis' headlights lit up his dark skin as he crossed in front of the car to reach her door. The warmth of his hand holding hers as he helped her out of his truck sent shivers through her body.

Soft footsteps trailed behind her.

"My alarm will go off once I open the door, we'll have to step inside quickly for me to shut it off," she said over her shoulder.

"Ok."

Once inside, LaKia shut off the alarm.

GIVE ME EVERYTHING

Standing behind her as she stood at her alarm keypad, Kendis said, "Thank you for going out with me tonight." His breath caused the hair on her shoulders to move. "I hope you had a good time. I know things have been kind of awkward between us. Part of that's my fault, I know. Plus our jobs don't help any..." Kendis stopped talking. Heat from his body told her he'd moved closer. "You don't want a casual relationship, and I don't know if I can be more right now. But, I know I want to know you better. Tell me what you want."

Paralyzed by her thoughts and feeling, she didn't know what to say. He'd admitted to her he didn't know if he could be anything more than what he was right now.

Whirling around to face him, her back pressed against the keypad. "I want everything. I want a man who desires me: mind, body, and soul. I don't want someone that only shares my bed, and nothing else." LaKia watched his eyes. Was she scaring him or was he listening. If she scared him away that would be fine. They could both move on. "I've had men take everything from me, my bo...everything. I don't want to give anything to anybody anymore if they don't want or can't give it back."

At some point during her rant, he'd moved closer. She arched her neck to look up into his eyes. Time stalled as she waited on him to say something. Each breath she inhaled scented with his cologne filled her lungs. She needed some space or else she might be tempted not to listen to his response, but kiss him, and break her own rules.

Sincerity in his eyes, he said, "LaKia, I don't want to hurt you, but I just got out of a real messed up situation."

Her cat, Jasper, cooed up to her ankles. Stepping aside, LaKia bent over to scoop him up. After a kiss and a few strokes of his fur, he bounced from her arms back to his favorite scratching post. The few moments allowed her to clear her mind. "What messed up situation?" She wanted to know.

"It's late. Maybe we should talk about this another time."

"So, you can ask the questions, but you can't answer them. Fine." LaKia began to walk to the door to open it and let Kendis out, but he stopped her.

Circling his arms around her waist from behind, he lowered his head until his cheek brushed against the side of her hair. He nuzzled his face into the side of her neck and kissed her tenderly. Drawing her into his body he whispered into her ear in a deep throaty voice, "LaKia, be patient. I'm thinking." He turned her towards him so he could look down into her face. Anger and hurt clouded her beautiful eyes. He didn't want her to be either. Even more, he didn't want to be the cause. He wanted her to listen to what he had to say.

Inhaling and exhaling deeply, he considered his words thoughtfully. "I moved to Ohio because while working on a project for my company, I met and fell in love with someone. I married her."

Holding her hand, he walked towards her sofa. He pulled her down beside him.

Without thinking, using his thumb and forefinger he began at the divot under his nose spreading the two fingers out in opposite directions bringing them down to his mouth, he started over each time he reached the corners of his mouth.

His hand dropped to his lap, and he kept talking, "We only knew each other for about six months before we got married, and we were married for three years. We were never apart. Wherever my job sent me, she would fly out and meet me. She'd stay for weeks at a time. There were only a few weekends when I was away for the Marine Corps reserves, when she couldn't visit me. But that was enough."

"Enough for what?"

"She cheated on me, with one of my buddies. But I didn't find out, then. One day she walked into our bedroom after showering, and told me we were pregnant. Family means everything to me. I wanted children before she did. I thought I had the perfect woman, and we were finally beginning our family. When she gave birth to my daughter, I was there. Watching my baby come into the world. For one year..." Kendis covered his face with both hands and sat, silently.

Kendis searched her eyes. In them he saw pity, but even in the low light he could see their slight shimmer. She held back her tears for him and listened.

"For one year, I thought Keisha was my daughter, but...she wasn't."

With his last words she kissed him, gentle and caringly, but he couldn't handle the touch of her lips to his in that moment. He wanted to taste her deeply. The urges inside of him grew stronger with each taste. He deepened the kiss. Every thrust grew more feral, and he probed desperately for more of her.

He raised his hands sifting his fingers through her soft tresses. As he leaned his body into hers, she gave way to his weight sinking into the cushions beneath her. They stretched lengthwise across the couch. He wanted her and his body couldn't hide it.

As his urgency grew, he pushed his body into hers. He could hear her breathing quicken and take on an unpredictable rhythm. He slid his hand under her blouse searching for her bra. It had no straps. He pulled it down and raised her arms above her head removing her blouse as he did. She lay under him exposed. Her breasts to his delight were just as he had imagined. They sat perfectly shaped—round and firm, her swollen nipples waited for his tongue. He took her nipple into his mouth, slowly circling and teasing until his desire overwhelmed him.

To be sure of what his next move should be, he looked into her eyes, he could see she wanted him, but he hesitated. If this happened tonight then what? He wasn't sure he was ready for what this would mean to her. Would it mean the same to him? He wanted her, but he didn't want to make another mistake. Not with her. He kissed her and she opened to him. She allowed him to undo her zipper and use his fingers to learn her body. Her hand stroked his thigh. She tugged at his zipper; he stopped her. But he didn't want to stop. He wanted to know her body.

After letting his tongue and lips fondle her nipples until she squirmed, he slid down her body to the source of the fire. He removed her strappy sandals, then her pants, exposing a pair of lacy thongs. He inhaled her scent, deeply. On his exhale, his warm breath flowed over her body through her underwear. Using his fingers he pulled her panties to the side revealing her soft fold. As his tongue played, she raised her hips to his mouth. He pressed her body back into the cushions of the couch. His tongue teased her with a playful game of hide and seek, while his hands gently squeezed and tugged at her hard nipples.

Whimpering his name, LaKia lifted her hips off the couch again. Again, he pushed her back down to the couch. "Wait, baby".

In short time, Kendis could feel the tremble of her legs as he controlled her urgent requests for him to explore her deeper and harder. Continuing to use his mouth to stoke the flames centered around her tiny bud set her body on fire. On a moan, she exhaled, and sank heavily into the couch beneath her.

He covered her whole body with his until she stilled. He wanted to be inside of her. To feel her body move with his, but he didn't think he could handle that yet.

CHAPTER SEVEN

Lying in her bed hypnotized by the smooth white ceiling, LaKia couldn't stop thinking about what had happened the night before. The feel of a man close to her had been forgotten. For the first time in a long time, she didn't stop herself. But, she still puzzled over his desire to please, but not allow her to return the favor.

The secrets and pain he shared with here were true. In her soul she knew it.

For a year, he believed a lie. Shivering at the thought of him loving another woman, she sank down deeper into the comfort of her blankets. Would he ever really be able to trust women again? She wanted him to trust her.

As the phone beside her she popped open one eye to glance at the clock. 7:30 am in the morning on Sunday who would call? Kendis?

Sounding froggy, she answered, "Hello."

"Hey, why didn't you call me back the other day?"

Hazy, she questioned, "Huh."

"I left you a message at work on Friday."

"Ohh." She'd left work early for an afternoon of beauty in preparation for her date with Kendis, but she didn't tell Nichelle.

"What? You didn't get the message again?"

"No, plus I left early."

"Bermuda Triangle strikes again. Oh, well, wake-up. I'm on my way over. I'll pick up some bagels on my way. I want to hear everything."

"Ok."

She flipped over, hugged her pillow and fell back to sleep. The doorbell announced Nichelle and woke her.

She had given Nichelle a key to her condo when she bought it. The only reason she ever rang the doorbell was to give her time to hide the evidence—of a man. Until last night, there hadn't been much need for their signal. Three rings and she'd come bursting in like always. So, she didn't move from her bed when the bell rang.

"Tell me everything," yelled Nichelle.

Everything? No way. She would be the pages of Kendis' diary. The tighter she held his secrets to her heart, the more a part of her he became. Nichelle fell across her bed and waited. "We had a good time. It's been a long time since I've been out."

Rummaging through the bag of bagels, Nichelle said, "It's been forever."

She grabbed the bag and followed her nose until she found a cinnamon raisin treat. "Yeah, whatever. Maybe he would be someone I could start over with, but..."

With anticipation in her voice Nichelle asked, "But what?"

"Nothing."

"Nothing."

"I was just thinking about something."

"What? Tell me."

"You have got to be the nosiest person in the world."

Nichelle placed her hand to her chest, sat up in the bed and gasped. "Nosey, what me?"

They laughed as they stuffed small chunks of bagel into their mouths.

"So, what do you think? Do you like the man or what?"

"I do. I like a lot of things about him, but I'm just not sure." LaKia raked her fingers through her hair. After Kendis left last night, she dropped into bed without pinning her hair up. She had to look wild and crazy by the head. "We both have so much going on."

Who was she trying to convince, herself or Nichelle?

"Sooner or later you've got to take a chance on somebody."

"That's what's scary. What if I jump in with both feet, and he doesn't?"

"So, what do you want to do? Sit around afraid forever."

Jasper, her twenty-pound black and white shorthair jumped on the bed startling both of them. They broke out into laughter again.

I'm tired of being by myself, but I'm tired of the game, too. I'm scared Nichelle. What if..." her words slowly faded?

Nichelle's voice lowered and filled with compassion. "I know you are, but stop closing everyone out. Let it go."

Tears fell. She wanted to let it all go. She wanted to forget, but each time she tried something went wrong and it hurt more. The safest place was in her own space—alone. In that moment, she realized Kendis had protected her: on the rapids, he carried her to her tent, and last night she...she hadn't felt that close to a man at least not in that way ever.

"Terrence and Kendis have known each other for a long time. My husband thinks he'll be good for you. You trust Terrence don't you?"

99

To the dismay of her cat, she stopped stroking him, long enough to poke Nichelle in the leg. Wiping tears from her eyes, she said, "Of course, but it's hard to try again and our jobs are involved. What if my company loses and I have to move? What if we win and he's relocated somewhere else?"

"You can deal with whatever happens, when and if it happens. But at least give it a shot."

Everything her friend said made sense. But, there were so many buts. Last night they'd taken a big step. What next? Was she ready? What if he decided he didn't want her? It would've all been for nothing.

Through hooded eyes, Lakia navigated traffic. The rumble of the hazard strips beneath her tires jolted her back into her drive. The sight of Kendis' house relieved her. Work, Kendis, and her conscience kept her awake at night. Weeks had passed, the long hours and poor eating sucked the energy out of her. She needed some fresh ideas, but she had none. Kendis and his team made a really strong argument: her 50-year old mall only employed a fraction of the number of people of the new development. And she didn't want to think about their contribution through taxes. How could the council vote against it?

After the council meeting the day before, she'd wanted to discuss some of her concerns with Kendis. Probably a bad idea to catch him outside of the meeting at his car, but she needed to talk...to him. The cold reaction she received confused her. Everything in the meeting had gone his way. He should've been thrilled. Maybe, he didn't need her anymore...now that his team was winning.

On the approach of one of the lawyers from his office, she flipped around and strolled back to her own car. No need to be humiliated by both of them.

But, she'd raced through her day because he'd called to apologize, and she couldn't wait to see him. First, she said

"No." But, honestly, dinner for two at his place. Perfect. She'd sent him an email saying yes.

She sifted through the bag full of groceries she held. Wine, baguette bread, some of her favorite cheeses, and tuna steaks. In her mind, she pictured the two them in front of the fireplace he kept tempting her with during their phone calls. Wine. Fireplace. Kendis. Mmmm.

Where was he? The door swung open. Steak scented smoke floated into the hallway around a gorgeous Amazon. Maybe, she should ask her. The Amazon wore a pair of men's boxer shorts and slippers—where they his?—and a nearly see through camisole. What was this woman doing here? Why invite her for dinner?

"Hello," she said curtly.

Why was she always in a situation where women popped up out of nowhere? "Is Kendis home?"

"No." The woman stared emotionless. "Can I help you?"

"Do you know when he'll be home?" She shifted her bag of groceries from one hip to the other.

With curiosity in her voice, the woman said, "Not sure. Who are you?"

"LaKia," she wanted to scream. "You?"

Before she could say her name, an adorable little girl ran up to the woman dragging a teddy bear bigger than her by one of its paws. Someone had put a t-shirt on the bear that read, I love my Daddy.

With one hand resting on her hip, and the other clasping the small hand of the child standing beside her, she said, "Kim, Kendis' wife, and this is Keisha his daughter." She swooped Keisha into her arms and glared.

Daughter! Wife! What happened to the EX that goes in front of wife? LaKia didn't need to hear it to confirm it.

GIVE ME EVERYTHING

Why didn't Kendis tell her they were here? That would have stopped him from getting what he wanted. DAMN. She had left work early, maybe she missed a return email, but he could've called her to tell her not to show up at his house. Why did she show up at his house anyway? Stupid. Just because he made her feel...feel what anyway? Sooner or later something had to happen. She stood in front of this woman with a bag full of food. She wanted to run.

Kim kept talking, "Do you want me to tell Kendis anything?"

Turning to walk away, LaKia said, "Ki stopped by."

Kim smiled. "Okay."

She heard the door close behind her.

Damn, Kendis was late, but he'd tried to call LaKia to let her know. She didn't answer. Her car wasn't in the driveway, maybe she hadn't been there, yet. He'd have time to shower and shave before she got there.

He pictured the night ahead of him as he unlocked the side door. Smoke.

"Welcome home, baby." Kim handed him a burned steak with a side of overcooked broccoli.

"What the hell are you doing in my house?"

Keisha ran up to him. "Dada. Hungry." Kim sat her plate down for a second and picked up Keisha.

"Let mommy and daddy talk. We'll be downstairs in a minute." The moment Keisha's feet touched the ground, she disappeared.

"What are you doing here, Kim?" He watched her as she confidently strolled through his house in a pair of his boxers and slippers, eating. "How did you even get in?"

Halting at the top of the stairs leading to the basement, she removed the forkful of food from her mouth long enough to say, "You keep the key in the same place we did in our house. Oh yeah, by the way, Ki stopped by."

"LaKia?" His head started spinning. Did Kim answer the door the way she looked now in his clothes? "What did she say?"

She swallowed her mouthful of food. "Nothing, she said to tell you she stopped by."

"Kim, did you say anything to her? Did you make her leave?"

With an angelic smile on her face, she said, "No. I told her I was your wife."

"What? Why in the hell did you do that?"

"Because I am," yelled Kim.

"You were, and I loved you. But, you gave that up...when you slept with my best friend." His fist slammed against the wall beside him emphasizing the conviction of his words. "Get out of my damn clothes and get out." The argument brought Keisha upstairs from the basement dragging the teddy bear he'd won for her at King's Dominion.

Her cries calmed and angered him. But, he didn't want to scare her. Both stood watching and waiting. He combed through the house throwing everything he saw of Kim's into the suitcase she showed up with weeks ago. Kim trailed behind him proclaiming her love and how she'd made a mistake with Steve. The whole time, all Kendis could think about was how he'd been warned by a lot of people about Kim and her sisters. They were known for their love of money and men with money. But, he fell in love with her and mistakenly thought he made enough money for her. Hell, for all he knew Steve didn't either, but Steve had more than him.

Ignoring every word she said, Kendis interrupted his packing long enough to ask, "And was Keisha a mistake, too. A year of making me love her, was that a mistake?"

Kim didn't respond. She didn't show a sign of regret. Anger, but no regret. Returning to the kitchen, he grabbed his phone and called the first airline that came to mind. He bought two tickets for the first flight out of Baltimore.

He slammed the phone back into its cradle. "You're leaving in the morning at 7:45 am from BWI."

The door bounced in its frame behind him.

"You'll regret this. I get what I want," shouted Kim.

Vaulting to his car, he tried to get his thoughts together as he pointed it in the direction of Ki's condo. Damn. He should've told her. Now, he had to figure out what to say that wouldn't sound like he hid Kim.

He pulled his SUV up behind her car at the curbside. He knocked and called. Filled her machine with pleas for forgiveness, but they were unanswered.

Nothing.

If she would just listen to him, he could explain. He'd managed to make the woman he was falling in love feel like an idiot. He sat in front of her house, until he began to feel like a stalker, calling, but he didn't even see a curtain move.

Sitting in the park outside of the county council with Kendis felt strange to LaKia. For weeks, she'd ignored his calls, and avoided him at work. She'd had enough of men, him, treating her like an afterthought. She deserved better.

But, the touch of his hand around her waist, and the feel of his breath across her skin as he whispered "Please talk to me" had her sitting beside him in the gazebo in the middle of the courtyard surrounded by the changing season—fallen leaves on the ground and trees filled with the colors of autumn.

Slender pieces of white painted wood held the thick glass walls of the gazebo together. Fortunately, it was not cold. She hated to be cold, and in the winter it had to be frigid, but she imagined the snow-covered dome would be beautiful. Perfect for a wedding.

After catching her breath from their brisk walk through the courtyard, she asked, "Kendis, why are we here?"

What more could he say, she'd heard it all...at least part of it before she deleted each message. All the flowers he'd sent were still in her condo. There were so many she'd spread them throughout the house. Every time he called, she wanted to talk to him, but something inside wouldn't let her.

Crying herself to sleep every night was becoming old. She needed to move on.

"To talk." He stood and walked to search for something in the distance of the courtyard. He faced her, and leaned against the glass of the gazebo. "What's up with you LaKia?"

Guarded, she muttered, "What do you mean?"

"I've been trying to explain things to you for weeks. Did you listen to any of my messages or did you delete them all?"

"I listened to them...but I don't understand why you couldn't tell me your ex-wife was in town."

LaKia couldn't disguise the hurt in her voice. She didn't want to hide it. He'd dragged her here.

"I showed up at your house with an arm full of food and wine. I thought we were going to have a nice night at home, but then I get there and your ex answers the door in your underwear. What was I supposed to think? If you wanted her, you should've told me." Rubbing her eyes, she finished her statement with an exhale released a ton of pressure from her mind.

"Baby, I told you in my messages, I dropped her at a hotel. She took my spare key with her, and came back on her own. I didn't know. And I don't want her. She wanted me...my money. I dropped her at the airport the next morning. I came to your house that night to explain," He sat beside her. "The night we talked...the night I tasted you, I knew I wanted you. Holding you felt natural. I didn't want to let you go. I wanted you to know me, too."

Her vision blurred from tears. "Was that all you wanted...to know me?" Fear took over her. She wanted him to answer "No."

Frustration in his voice, he said, "That's not what I mean, and you know that. Don't play with my words. Let me finish...the reason I didn't' take it further was because of Kim and Keisha."

"If so, then why not tell me everything?"

"What? I haven't spoken to her since I took Keisha to Kings Dominion. I thought they were gone."

"I don't know...I guess...it hurt," she cried

"Baby, I'm sorry. What kind of man do you think I am?" He shook his head. "Never mind, I guess I know the answer to that. But, do you think I would let you walk into that type of situation?"

His last words seemed almost desperate. "I...I'm not sure." Over the past weeks, she'd felt incredibly lonely. It had been difficult not to answer the phone when he called, but she needed to protect herself. "I thought I knew, but she confused me."

"Was that the only reason you've been avoiding me? Nothing else?"

The pain in his eyes hurt her. She stared at the ground. "I felt used, Kendis. Stupid." She'd never experienced feelings like those their last night together. Since Derrick she'd been with other men, not many, but none of them held her or made her feel as desired and safe as Kendis.

"Look at me." Irritation showed on his face.

She wanted to believe him...every word and emotion. If she sat for a moment longer and listened, she would. Pushing herself up from the bench, she said, "Kendis, I've got to go. I've got a lot to do tonight."

Kendis watched as she stood to walk away from him. He hadn't poured his heart out to a woman since Kim. The wrong one. Now, that he had the right one, everything was blowing up in his face. She'd shut him out for weeks, and still tried. What was he missing?

He clutched her hand. "Whatever you're holding back from me, tell me. Why do you keep pulling away from me? We can make this work. Trust me."

"It doesn't matter."

"Aren't you tired of having your heart on lockdown?" He paused. "I am."

"I just want to go." The tremble in her hands vibrated through him. She watched his hand travel up her arm. When his hand reached the side of her face cradling her cheek, she cried. He held her.

Placing his hand under her chin, Kendis raised her head to an angle which allowed him to look down into her tear filled eyes. Her hair looked darker due to the lack of light filtering through the glass of the gazebo. Some of the auburn locks had found their way into her face. Brushing them away, he could see into her eyes as never before, round in shape and hazel with little green flecks. They were sad and definitely hiding something from him.

She closed her eyes, and he kissed both eyelids. Moving down her face he brushed lightly over the bridge of her nose down to her full lips. He kissed her. Kissing her piqued his manhood. He didn't want to break away, but containing the passion growing inside of him would be difficult if he waited any longer. Kissing her would not get him the answers he sought. Pulling away from her, he didn't let go of his grip on her body. He held her waist firmly because he was afraid she might run if he didn't.

They sat side by side.

"Start at the beginning."

"The beginning? I don't know if there is a beginning..." trailing off LaKia seemed to be searching for words. She began again. "My college boyfriend and I..."

With each word, Kendis' anger increased. Every nerve in his body flamed. Each and every muscle wanted to crush Derrick Jones. Motionless and wordless, he listened. He watched her mouth as each word escaped. He wanted to hold her, kiss her, and make love to her, to show her how gentle and loving it can...no should be, but he kept his distance. As she told him her story a volcano inside of Kendis erupted, he counted each tear, promising himself that if he ever ran into Derrick Jones he'd shed as many as she had cried that night.

"I don't know if it was because of the girls grinding against him on the dance floor, the drinks, his boys or what? But that night he didn't care what I said or did. I scratched, kicked, and bit him, but he kept doing what he was doing."

"Baby, I don't know what to say."

The thoughts going through his mind were dizzying. There were so many questions. If she was in college when this happened...was she...a virgin?

Breathless, LaKia stopped talking. She wrung her hands in her lap as a waterfall of tears streamed down her face.

"Since then, I seem to keep making mistakes with men. They never seem to just want me. All of me. And you...you have so much in common with him. Basketball playing fraternity guy..."

"Stop. Don't compare me to him. I'm not the same guy. I wouldn't do that to you."

"I didn't say that...I just meant that you..."

"You meant what? Nothing. I'm not like him."

"I know."

Holding her hand, Kendis said, "You were young...in college. Were you a virgin?"

The tears that had finally stopped now gushed down her cheeks.

"Yes."

Rising from beside her, Kendis paced the floor. Scanning the gazebo he searched for something to punch, but there wasn't anything. She looked nervous. He tried to calm down. He didn't want her to be afraid, not of him.

As the sunset and night fell, they sat quietly for hours. Kendis had kicked his leg across the bench straddling it, allowing LaKia to stretch out her legs and nuzzle up into his body. He draped his arms around her, and she rested against his chest. Feeling the warmth of her body flowing into his, Kendis felt whole. He didn't want to let her go. Where she was now is where he wanted her to remain forever: in his arms, in his heart, in his life.

Silently, he prayed he never ran into Derrick Jones.

CHAPTER EIGHT

Lakia smoothed a hand down the length of her body as she answered the door. Prompt as always, Kendis tempted her just on the other side. Her jealousy piqued by the gold sweater that hugged his solid chest. The jeans he wore didn't give away anything about the surprise hiding behind that zipper. A surprise because after months of dating he regarded her like a nun recently escaped from a convent.

The passion still existed, but no action. He soothed her with a list of reasons why they should be sure before they made that move. When she wanted men to leave her alone, they didn't. But, this man's subtle rejections increased her desire and love. Remembering the way his tongue playfully caressed every inch of her body brought it alive. Her nipples responded to her thoughts awakening the ache between her legs that longed for his touch. She needed a drink or something to take her mind off the man in front of her. "Do you need anything before we leave?"

"No, I'm good."

"Well then, let's go see what Nichelle has up her sleeve." A double date with her best friend would definitely take her mind off ripping off his clothes with her teeth.

"Wait a minute."

She had her purse and keys. Did she forget something? "What?"

Smiling mischievously, he asked, "Can I have a kiss?"

GIVE ME EVERYTHING

Wrapping her arms around his neck she leaned in to peck him on the lips. His hands slid up her thighs and rested just above her hips. Too close to where she'd love them to stay. They didn't move; he held on and drew her into him.

If she stayed in his arms any longer, she wouldn't let him walk away tonight like he had every other night. As she pulled away, she used the door to steady herself. He searched her eyes and she smiled. They needed to leave before she pulled him inside and shackled him to her headboard.

The candles of the small restaurant casted dancing shadows along the length of the walls. Nichelle and Terrence sat tucked away in a corner and they joined them.

As they approached the table both rose from their chair to greet them.

"Hey man."

"What's up?" Mirroring Terrence's exactly—the two men in fluid motion tapped the top and bottom of each other's fist.

"Hey, sweetie," Nichelle said as she kissed LaKia on the cheek.

"Hey, girlie," LaKia replied.

Both Kendis and Terrence assisted the women with their chairs as they sat.

Dinner began simply enough. The topic of conversation was not Kendis and LaKia. But, LaKia knew it wouldn't last for long. The etouffe in front of her usually disappeared immediately, but she didn't have a big appetite, tonight. She had refused to give Nichelle the information she begged to know by phone. What had they been doing? Where had they been going? Had they done this or that? Where they going to this or that? Out of fear or because of a weird belief in jinxing something good she never revealed anything.

Nichelle agreed to stop asking questions. But, would she keep that promise over dinner?

Nichelle grabbed her purse with one hand, and LaKia's wrist with the other. "Excuse us guys." Rising from her seat as she spoke, Nichelle gave LaKia no time to do anything but snatch her own purse from the table.

As LaKia stood at the small pedestal sink in the ladies room reapplying her lip-gloss, she waited for a barrage of questions. .

Nichelle didn't disappoint as she burst from the stall. "So girl, tell me what's up."

Busying herself by poking around in her purse, she didn't look at her friend. "Nothing. Everything is good."

"Good? How?" Touching up her own lips, Nichelle cocked her head to one side as if preparing to analyze every word uttered by her.

"He's a good man, but there are so many things to consider..."

Nichelle's lip-gloss slipped from her hand and clinked against the porcelain sink. She tried to catch the tube as it rolled from side to side. "You told him!"

How'd she know that! "Yes, I didn't want to...I didn't mean to, but I did." Nichelle would never let it go now. Sometimes, like now, she regretted telling her best friend about that night long ago.

"How did he respond?"

"I think it scared him a little. Now, he's almost afraid to touch me like I might break or something."

Placing one hand on each of LaKia's shoulders Nichelle stopped her from turning away. Her friend's unshakeable stare penetrated her.

"He's just trying to be considerate."

"I know. But, what do I do?"

Letting go of LaKia's shoulders, Nichelle hugged her and said, "It was a long time ago, but it still affects you. So, give him time to get used to it, too."

"I'm trying, but geez, it is hard watching him leave every night."

With one arched eyebrow raised, Nichelle smiled. "Horny much? So, what else you two been doing?"

"Hanging out, movies, dinners. He's an awesome cook." She patted her stomach. "I think I've gained a few pounds since I met him."

"Getting to know each other. That's good." Then in the next breath, she said, "Sounds like you need to have a par-tay at your house to showcase your man's cooking," with a hint of mischievousness in her voice Nichelle winked at LaKia as she spiked her spunky hair to give it more volume.

"I don't know about that one," she laughed. Taking a moment to give herself the once over one more time, she gave her reflection a nod of approval before they exited the ladies' room.

Kendis relaxed into the cushions of the driver's seat. The hard part was over.

He watched as LaKia tucked her jacket around herself hiding her hands inside the sleeves. With a few punches of the temp button, he turned up the heat.

After the ladies returned to the table, the evening had taken on a noticeably more relaxed feel. Nichelle had to know about Derrick. Eventually, he would have to work up the nerve to ask her a few more questions. Did he hurt LaKia? Had she seen him since college? There were so many questions he wanted to have answered. But, he didn't want to hurt her in any way...including her memories.

Not knowing the answers screwed his world because half the damn time he didn't know what the hell to do. Self-control faded away each time he kissed or held her.

Turning onto LaKia's street, Kendis patted her thigh to wake her from her nap. The softness of her skin caressed his palm as his hand stroked up and down her thigh reacquainting itself with every curve. "LaKia, wake up baby, you're home."

She rubbed her cheek against her shoulder as she slowly opened her eyes. Watching her, Kendis remembered one of the things he loved about her. She could be a fierce woman when she needed to be, but her delicate nature attracted him most. Gazing into her eyes as she woke he wanted to protect her from everything and everybody. How could a man say he loved a woman then hurt her?

He didn't want to hurt her, but he barely had it together. His ex had screwed his best friend, and lied about his child. But, Derrick had violated LaKia. Every moment, he fell more in love with her, but it's easy to lose control when you're deep inside of a woman. Not like he was some kind of an animal, but shit hearing her voice on the phone made his body want her.

Yawning, she sat up in her seat and asked, "We're here already? That was quick."

Briefly taking his eyes off the driveway in front of him to look into her eyes, he said, "So, now I know I can't feed you and expect much afterwards."

"You don't have to worry about me, I can handle my food."

"Says who?" With a lighthearted laugh, Kendis got out of the car to help LaKia with her door.

Walking up to her front door, he didn't want to think about leaving. After his split from Kim whenever he went out with a woman he took full advantage of their generosity. He would definitely expect to be invited in and served breakfast in the morning—if he stayed that long.

Pausing at her door with her back to him, she asked, "Are you staying tonight?" She opened her door and rushed to the alarm to shut it off.

Hanging back in the doorway, Kendis stretched out his arms to LaKia and said, "Come here baby." If he stood there one more moment it would take nothing for this woman to change his mind. He had decided not to stay. Holding her as they slept would feel good, but it wouldn't be enough.

Dragging her feet at the alarm keypad, LaKia walked toward him. "You're not going to stay are you? Why?"

"I think I should go home tonight."

He held her tightly to his chest, she could barely move.

"But why? I thought we had a good time. Don't you want to spend the night with me?"

"It has nothing to do with you. Of course I want to be with you tonight, but..."

Kendis didn't know what to say. He didn't have a lot of time to figure it out. She cut him off when she tore away from his grip.

"You don't have to stay if you don't want to." Removing her coat she walked toward the closet. In a wooden, distant voice, LaKia muttered indistinctly, "Close the door behind you as you leave."

Kendis' thoughts twisted in knots as he watched her walk up the stairs to her bedroom. Hypnotized, he couldn't take his eyes off her as she climbed the narrow staircase with slow sultry steps. She skimmed the index finger of her left hand along the wooden railing. Briefly, she hesitated to straighten a shadowbox frame containing an African tribal mask, but then she continued up the stairs.

She knew he loved her ass, and gave him plenty of time to think about it.

He could feel his erection press against the zipper of his pants as he watched the sway in her hips. The wool-like fabric of her red wrap dress swayed with her body as her small bowed hips rocked side to side. Damn. He could have her out of that dress and beneath him with a slight tug of that bow at her waist. Every night he left her hard as a rock. Restless nights filled with dreams of her woke him, often, with a need to hop into a cold shower to clear his head and calm his body.

Closing the door, Kendis walked toward the stairs. When he got to his destination, he didn't know what he would do, but he couldn't leave her again tonight.

LaKia's dress hung open exposing the lacy underwear she'd bought with him in mind when she glanced up to see Kendis standing in her bedroom doorway. His eyes roamed her body. She let the dress slip from her shoulders to the floor around her, and he responded.

Before another thought ran through her mind he had her in his arms. Melting like butter into each other's embrace he deeply kissed her and she responded with equal desire. The touch of his hands, his mouth wasn't enough. She needed more. She pulled and tugged at his clothes.

Something in her head snapped and she shoved Kendis away, she couldn't catch her breath, and panicked. Who did he think he was? One second he had one foot out of the door and the next he stood in her bedroom.

Stepping away from him, she looked into his eyes. Searching for an answer as to why he had this sudden change of mind. Seeing the desire in his eyes, she knew if he touched her again she would dissolve. "What are you doing here? I thought you were leaving."

"I changed my mind."

GIVE ME EVERYTHING

In a cracking voice, LaKia asked, "Why?"

"I should never have tried to leave."

Beaming, LaKia felt her feet move beneath her carrying her closer. The space between them—her safety net—slowly disappeared.

His every touch burned deeper and deeper into her soul. He ran his tongue slowly over his lips, and then he leaned down and kissed her.

He cast her bra to the floor, and cupped her breasts in his hands. A gentle squeeze of her nipples sent a little tingle through her body. She reached for his head, and brought his mouth to her breasts. The touch of his tongue to her nipples elicited a sigh. The more he sucked the wetter she got.

One of his hands moved up her neck, her head fell back allowing him to kiss her. Sliding his other hand down her hips, he pulled at the string of the thong she wore. He released her. Obeying his silent request, she slipped out of the delicate panty.

Unzipping his jeans, he stripped them and his boxer briefs off in one swift motion. Stiff and rigid the length of his shaft filled the space between them. Pausing briefly, he reached for the condom he kept in his wallet and rolled it along the length of his manhood.

With one hand he slowly stroked himself, allowing LaKia to have full view of his body, he asked, "Do you like what you see?"

Running her hands through her hair, she smiled in response to the question and nodded.

Holding her against his naked body, he allowed her head to rest on his chest. She trembled in his embrace. "Baby, tell me what you want me to do. I don't want to hurt you."

"Do you love me?"

He kissed her soft and deep. "I love you because after everything, you're taking a chance. Trusting me with your heart..." Stretching his arm down to her side, he lifted her right leg creating enough room to allow his right leg to nestle between hers. She held her leg in that position, wrapping it around his hard buns. "...and your body."

His talented fingers explored her body, and then he slowly slid in and out of her. Finally, when she wanted him the most, he thrust himself completely into her. She gasped.

"Are you okay...did I hurt you?"

Grabbing his bottom with both hands, she pulled him deeper into her. "I'm fine."

"Do you want me to..."

"Don't stop."

Covering her mouth with his, his kiss explored her neck trailing down her body until his mouth rested on one of her swollen nipples.

"Give me more."

"I've wanted you for so long." He lifted her off her feet, and thrust deeper inside of her. Her body bounced up and down in the air as he plunged deeper and deeper. Again and again, he brought her body down to meet his. Her kisses deepened barely giving them time to breathe.

He threw her onto the bed beside them, and repositioned himself above her. Could it be possible for him to fill her more? Each stroke brought something inside her to life. "There...there..."

He gently played with her nipples. Her back rose, slightly, from the bed beneath her. She didn't ever want him to stop. She pulled him in deeper and he swiveled his hips increasing the intensity of desire building inside her. No longer could she control her body. Little tremors rolled through her body. "Kendis..." Her quivering body excited his.

GIVE ME EVERYTHING

With each clamp of her body around his, he grew harder and thicker.

"Grab my ass, and pull me in deeper," he commanded.

She did and he kissed her hard. She couldn't breathe. His rhythm sped up, and then he hovered above her, firmly grinding his body deeply into hers. "You're so wet. You feel so good," he moaned. "Mmm, I'm about to cum."

She felt his penis throb inside of her. It felt so good. Slowly, she rolled her hips. She wanted him again. He rested his head in the crook of her neck.

After the waves rolling through his body stopped, she nibbled at his ear and whispered, "Let's do that again?" then laughed.

CHAPTER NINE

Unfolding himself from his car, Kendis stretched out to the full length of his 6'2" frame. Pushing up the sleeve of his jacket to check the time, a rush of heat ran through his body as he realized he'd left his watch at LaKia's house. Standing at his car door, he had to stop himself from jumping behind the wheel and driving back for another round.

What had she whispered into his ear? He thought about it with a smile on his face...he had been ready for round two and three. He'd been ready for a long time.

He glanced up at the tower across the street from his building. Shit, he was late. It took a little longer to drive in from LaKia's house than it did his. Remember that for the future. Plus, LaKia wouldn't let him leave this morning without a morning quickie and he was more than willing to serve her.

The smell of vanilla and hazelnut called his name. He popped into the kitchen for a quick glass before he joined the meeting.

Before he could take his first sip something disturbed him. The sharp clicks of expensive Italian shoes against the wood floor grew louder. Larry Dukes, a small, fat man who'd worked for his company since before Kendis was born strolled up to him. The look on Larry's face, conspiratorial in nature—made Kendis ill at ease.

"Kendis how was your weekend?"

GIVE ME EVERYTHING

After taking a sip of his coffee, he responded, "Good. What about you?"

"Great, I came into the office on Sunday. I had hoped I would see you here. I had a great idea about the Eastover case."

Larry had not been quiet about his objections to Kendis as lead on the Eastover project. From what Kendis heard, Larry had tried every brown-nosing tactic he could think of to get the lead chair. That man wanted to make partner, and would sell his soul to do it.

Kendis avoided most conversations with Larry because he was an all-around ass. Whatever he had planned, Kendis didn't want to be a part of it. Lawyers like Larry were why most people thought Lawyers were shady.

He didn't really care about Larry's idea. He led this project, not Larry. "A great idea, what?"

"LaKia Jackson. Are you involved with her?" Larry smiled with complete pride in his line of questioning, without waiting for a response, he continued, "We could use your relationship to our advantage. If you're a team player."

"Team player?" Kendis wanted to hit him. He couldn't without losing his job, but he wanted to tell him LaKia was not a toy to be played with by him or anyone. He wanted to tell him he loved with her, but he couldn't.

"Yeah, team player. I've seen you together a couple of times: in the parking lot and in the gazebo. I've got it on good authority the two of you are a couple. I think she would do anything you asked."

Attempting to keep his voice empty of anger, he asked, "Good authority? What does that mean?"

Larry smirked, but didn't respond.

Glaring at Larry, Kendis spoke in a slow cautious manner narrowing the gap between them. "What do you want me to ask her to do?"

Larry took a few wary steps backwards. "Ask her to back off. Ask her to use her influence on the merchants at her property to talk to us. That property is old. We could work out a deal to have most of her merchants have a location at the new Eastover site, of course at a higher rent. But, there's no need for her to know that. If she works on the small stores, and we work on the national stores we can make sure we don't lose the momentum we've built up."

Inside his mind he imagined himself walking up to the short shifty man and pulling him up by the collar until his legs dangled beneath him, but he didn't. Instead he said, "What makes you think she would do that for me?"

"It's obvious that she's in love with you. Besides, my source tells me the two of you spend a lot of time together."

Source? This was the second time the bulbous man had mentioned someone giving him information. How did his source know so much about what happened between LaKia and him? Shit, it didn't matter. The one thing he knew, it didn't come from them, so it could be denied.

"Larry, there's no love involved. We have mutual friends." Kendis took another sip of his coffee. The smile on Larry Dukes' face slowly morphed into a confused surprise.

He pushed past Larry knocking him against the counter behind him. "Larry, stay out of my damn personal life. This is my project. I'm lead, not you. Your source should talk to me, and I'll give them the facts."

"Kendis, we need this."

"We don't, and I'm late for a meeting."

Kendis could feel Larry's stare cutting into his back as he walked to his office. He hoped this would be the end of it, but the feeling in his gut told him Larry wouldn't let it be that easy.

The day had been filled with project updates and conference calls, but Kendis still kept an eye out for Larry. He didn't have much respect for the man, but the guy wouldn't have the office or salary he did if he didn't have the respect of somebody.

Business was business, but Kendis took a lot of pride in the way he handled his projects. And, as long as, he had the results the company wanted, they left him alone to do it his way. He kept everything above board and had never made any sort of agreement or arrangement he believed remotely questionable. Now, he had a co-worker approach him about using sexual influence over a woman. A woman he had fallen in love with. What if he took his boneheaded idea to somebody else?

Kendis decided he needed to leave before he went to find Larry and kick his ass for asking him something so damn stupid. As he stood to head towards his door it flung open slamming against the wall behind it.

Carl Fitzsimmons, Vice President of Acquisitions. Right behind him, Larry with a conspicuous grin on his face.

Apologizing for making such noise with the door, Carl said, "Kendis I guess I don't know my own strength." He continued, "Do you have a moment? Larry brought an interesting idea to me earlier today."

Larry shifted his body, which hid his orbed frame from Kendis' gaze behind Carl's massive girth.

Echoing Carl from his hidden position, Larry said, "Great idea."

Kendis felt like leaping across his desk. But, instead, he took his cue from and returned to his desk chair. Carl pulled up a chair and forced his full girth into it. Larry slid his chair slightly closer to Carl and sat.

Devoid of emotion, he asked, "Carl, are we talking about the same idea Larry mentioned to me this morning?"

Carl's smile broadened as he nodded his head in agreement with Kendis' statement.

"Carl, what makes you think sex will work?"

"Because of Larry's comments. He said it's blatantly obvious she's in love with you. And we all know how you are with the ladies," he laughed. "I think it's a great idea, unless of course...you've fallen in love with her, too."

The room fell silent. A soft hum generated by Kendis' computer filled the air. Both men were waiting on an answer from Kendis, who shot his glance back and forth between the two men trying to decide who to snatch up first. If he was in love with her it wasn't any of their damn business.

Responding carefully, Kendis said, "In love...I think she is intelligent and definitely sexy, but..."

He couldn't finish his statement before Carl jumped in to make his own. "Good then, it's settled, you and Larry work on this idea. And let me know how it progresses." Ungluing the chair from his body, Carl stood at the door before Kendis could respond to his order. He examined Kendis from the entryway. "I don't have to remind you the bonus on this project will be considerable."

With that statement, Carl left and Larry remained in Kendis' office alone. Before Kendis could move, Larry scrambled from his chair and quickly disappeared down the corridor behind Carl.

Kendis' elbows dug into his oak desk as he sat resting his head in his hands. The tones from the clock tower across the street told him he the lateness of the hour. He'd sat at his desk for hours doing nothing. Serenity eluded him. He didn't know what to do, but he couldn't do what they wanted, no chance in hell. But, what about his job—career? No job, no house, no woman—LaKia. If he could talk to her, he knew she'd help him lay out a plan, but she'd also feel responsible for his situation, and she wasn't. Larry created the problem, and when everything was over, he'd make sure Larry burned for his part.

He picked up the phone and called Terrence. Even if he called him a coward, at least it would be coming from Terrence—not LaKia.

Kendis lost count of the number of times the phone rang, but as he was about to hang up Terrence answered the line.

"Hello."

"Hey, man... Kendis here. Can you get out of the house for a minute?"

"What's up?"

The phone lines at Brady could be listened in on from other offices. Aware of this, Kendis didn't want to go into any sort of detail on the phone. "I just need to run something by you."

With concern in his voice, Terrence replied, "What?"

"I don't want to talk about it on the phone, but I need some advice."

"Okay, how about that sports bar on the harbor?"

"Cool."

Kendis pulled into the parking lot, and grabbed his cell. He considered calling Terrence to cancel, but he needed to talk to somebody. He knew what he should do, but he could stand to lose everything. He snatched his key out of the ignition, and headed towards the bar.

Terrence at the bar. Perfect. He could use a drink. As he approached, he caught the bartender's eye and asked for Hennessey straight before he sat on the empty barstool next to Terrence.

"Kendis, man what's up?"

For a moment, he could only stare at the liquid in his glass. Mesmerized, he swirled his glass of Hennessey in slow wide circles. "I don't know man."

"You dragged me out. Spit it out."

"Larry Dukes and Carl FitzSimmons came into my office today with a crazy ass scheme." Swallowing hard, he continued, "They want me to sleep with LaKia in order to get her to play for our team."

Anger flared in eyes as wide as saucers, and then Terrence dropped his beer bottle to the bar. "What the fuck? Did you tell them to back the hell off?" Terrence took another sip from his bottle. "Better yet, tell them you quit."

Temper soaring, Kendis said, "Quit, man, you know how hard I've worked for this."

Shock on his face, Terrence stared at Kendis. "I thought you said you were in love with her?"

"I...I'm not saying I'm going to do it. I'm just trying to figure out what I can do."

Drinking from the fresh Heineken the bartender placed in front of him, Terrence said, "Be a man, tell them to kiss your ass."

"Damn, Bro don't you think I know that. But my parents worked their asses off to put me through school. I can't lose it like this." Kendis' anger grew—Carl, Larry, Terrence, everybody.

Slamming his fist on the bar, Terrence said, "While they worked their asses off to get you here I know they taught you better than this."

Terrence's words sent a shiver of shame through him. "I'm not trying to roll over and take it. But, shit, we don't deserve to lose everything because their asses think they can play around with other people's lives."

This time taking a long drink from his beer, Terrence said, "Let me think about this for a minute."

"I've been thinking about this all day."

With a questioning look on his face, slowly Terrence said, "How did he know about you and LaKia?"

Larry admitted to seeing them together, but he kept referring to a source. Kendis had been careful on the phone. They'd only spoken a few times by phone from his office. His nosey assed secretary couldn't have eavesdropped.

"He saw us together a couple of times, plus he says he's got some source."

Terrence gulped his beer. "Meddlesome bastard. It sounds like he's got some sort of a spy."

"I know. Maybe, my secretary, but I don't know. Maybe I could tell him she's got a man, or that I've already slept with her and she caught me with someone else and hates me."

"I don't think the first one will work. They know you're a player, they're not gonna go for that. But they might believe she hates you."

"Whatever I decide their source will probably be watching me. I wouldn't be able to hang out with her. Unless..." Kendis' thoughts roamed.

"Unless what?"

"We involve the ladies, and I run a little scheme of my own."

"Huh?" Terrence's mouth hung open as he said, "Tell LaKia and Nichelle?"

"Yeah."

"I don't know about that one, unless you're going to tell them everything," said Terrence pensively.

"No, listen to what I'm saying. They want me to run a scheme on LaKia. What if I flip the script and we run a scheme on them?"

"What kind of a scheme and how does it keep you from being blacklisted all around town."

"I don't know yet, but what if I get the drop on them."

"We've got to tell LaKia and Nichelle as much as possible."

"If we tell them everything, whatever we do won't seem as believable. They'll be watching LaKia to see how she reacts to what I'm doing. Shit, but if I don't tell her..." Kendis hung his head down to his chest and shook his head.

Agreeing with Kendis' unspoken words, Terrence said, "True, true."

When Terrence left, Kendis stayed behind. He wanted to think, and that would be hard at home. He knew LaKia would have called by now. The thought of hearing her voice sent a wave of nausea through his body. He wanted to tell her everything, but what would she think? Would she think he was a jerk for dragging his feet? Would she want to be a part of his plan?

Aside from LaKia, Kendis' father kept running through his head. He couldn't forget the words his father said at his graduation from law school. "Thurgood Marshall made my father proud, but you make me proud."

But like Terrence said, his parents raised him better, and his father would be disappointed if he didn't protect his woman. He hadn't worked out how, but he did have a good idea.

GIVE ME EVERYTHING

The black letters on the Kendis' computer screen blurred. He waited for Larry to slither into his office. He wasn't sure when he would show up. He watched over his shoulder all day half-expecting Larry to jump out of every shadowed corner he walked past. But he didn't. The day was almost over, and he hadn't seen any sign of him. He'd spoken with Terrence earlier in the day, and they'd begun to put their half-developed plan together.

Terrence told Nichelle Kendis had problems at work. He'd explained to her the partners were putting pressure on Kendis to participate in a plan to deceive the merchants at LaKia's property. And he told LaKia the same thing, but he added that he didn't want to tell her more because he didn't want anyone to say she'd been involved. They'd both decided this would be enough to get the ladies involved, and cover their asses when they filled them in on everything later.

The click of Italian shoes put him on his guard. Larry Dukes stood in his entryway. "Hello, Kendis."

Slowly, Kendis ended his planning and focused on controlling his temper. Lifting his eyes from his computer screen. "I'm in."

Larry smiled and disappeared as quickly as he'd appeared.

At dinner, Kendis could barely deflect LaKia's relentless bombardment of questions. He knew she desperately wanted to know what his company wanted him to do. He kept to what he and Terrence planned and limited his response.

Uneasiness in her voice, her brow furrowed as she said, "Kendis, if you tell me what's going on, maybe I can help."

"Baby, I know you want to help, but I need to handle this. To protect you."

"I know you say that is the best way, but...maybe, together we can figure out how to protect me and help you?"

Damn, he loved her.

He should have told those pricks to take their damn job and keep it. But, he didn't know anybody that could take care of a wife and family on good intentions. That was the beauty of the simple plan he and Terrence had created. Get proof of what his partners wanted, so they wouldn't stop him with bad references when he quit. He just needed enough time to get another job and get proof of their actions to cover his ass.

"Kendis, Kendis?"

"Sorry, baby, I was lost in thought there for a minute."

"Kendis if you won't talk to me how am I supposed to help?"

He fixed his eyes on hers across the glass-topped dinette table. "You're helping me now. You're here with me."

Fretfully, she leaned back in her chair and folded her arms across her body. "You know what I mean."

Rising from his chair, Kendis walked around the small table in LaKia's dining room to where she sat. Dragging her chair out, he bent over and picked her up.

"Is this supposed to make me forget you won't talk to me?"

"No, it's to let you know I've fallen in love with you."

She tightened her arms around his neck and kissed his cheek slowly dragging her tongue along his neck as he carried her towards the stairs.

"Unless you want me to lay you down on these steps, you'd better stop."

She kissed him again, this time slow and soft biting gently at his bottom lip. He felt his manhood harden and stiffen against his slacks. He stopped where he stood in the middle of the slender stairwell leading up to the second level of her condo.

GIVE ME EVERYTHING

He wanted her right there. He didn't want to wait. She stretched her legs to the step beneath her. Quietly, she waited. Kendis maneuvered around her and sat on the step. Slowly, LaKia raised her skirt and agilely removed her underwear allowing Kendis to watch. He fondled the soft auburn curls between her legs. Then he leaned forward, and replaced his hand with his mouth. She placed both hands on either side of his head, and slowly moved her body along his tongue. He latched onto her clit, and she froze. Letting him taste her.

She knelt before him and stroked the bulge in his pants with her hand. She unzipped his slacks and assisted him in removing them. While he searched his pockets for a condom, she played with the tip of his penis with her tongue. With a rhythm that damn near made him come, she used her hands and mouth to make him thick and hard.

He rolled the condom along the length of his rod, and she turned her back to him and lowered herself into the cradle of his legs. Slowly, she slid her body down until he felt the wetness of her body engulf him. She ground her body into his making his body ache and become more rigid inside of her.

He reached underneath her blouse, unhooking the clasp of her bra. Eagerly, he searched for her nipples. When he found them they were hard and firm between his fingers. He massaged and tweaked them until she moaned from pleasure. Guiding his hands, she placed them between her legs. She squeezed her legs together and her moans grew louder. Her moans heightened his excitement and his thrusts became stronger going deeper with each stroke.

Turning her head toward Kendis, she caught her bottom lip between her teeth then quickly released it before she whispered to him, "Baby, I'm there...more."

He placed a hand on each of her hips and pulled her body into his one last time. In unison they both exploded.

CHAPTER TEN

As LaKia twisted the knob of her office door she had her mind on her night with Kendis. Again, she leaned down to massage the dull throb in her thigh. It was fun making them sore. She laughed out loud as she sauntered into her office.

The day flew past. She hadn't realized it was lunchtime until Kendis called and asked her to meet him. She hadn't planned on going out for lunch, but she'd gotten a lot of work done; she could treat herself to the pleasure of a lunch date.

Driving over to Kendis' office she couldn't stop herself from running various scenarios against Eastover through her head. What could they possibly want him to do that he would be so worried about her? As she pulled up in front of Kendis' building she saw him standing out front with two men. From his posture, she recognized Larry Dukes from town meetings. But, the other figure wasn't familiar. As she approached them, Kendis broke away from the two men and headed in her direction. He hid her from their view as he draped his body over hers capturing her mouth in his. It may have been her imagination, but it felt like he covered her in a protective shield. She didn't think he would ever let her go.

Catching hold of her hand, he guided her in the direction of the two men. He let her hand go just long enough for her to greet them. As he finished his conversation, he wrapped his arm around her waist to guide her back to the parking lot.

Carl stopped them.

GIVE ME EVERYTHING

"LaKia, we're having a small dinner party at the Crosstown Country Club next week. We're on opposite sides of this deal, but we don't have to be enemies. You should join us."

Examining Kendis before answering, she replied, "Well, if you're inviting me, I would love to attend."

Pleased by her response, Carl shook Kendis' hand as he stated, "I'm glad to see you've made a good choice."

Gesturing with a subtle nod of his head, Kendis said, "Always, sir. Always."

LaKia thought the exchange cryptic. She assumed it had something to do with whatever shady things they'd asked Kendis to do. Had he agreed to do what they wanted? She embraced Kendis' waist in a reciprocal move to his as they turned to walk away.

She stretched her neck to whisper into his ear. "I think your boss likes me. That's good for us, right?"

A quick glance behind her confirmed that Carl and Larry watched as they walked to Kendis' car. He stopped. Then turned to face her and said, "It wouldn't matter to me if he didn't." The force of his kiss caused her to stagger from its power.

LaKia never paid a lot of attention to gossip at work, but this time she couldn't walk away. As she silently sat in the ladies' bathroom, she couldn't ignore the voices of the two women as they bounced off the walls and echoed in her ears. The first woman's voice she recognized. Amy Poole. If this were high school, Amy Poole would be the high school gossip that spread rumors to be cool. The other voice she couldn't make out. She peeped through the crack in the door of the stall, but she didn't think she knew her.

Tall, slim, light-skinned woman with long jet-black hair. She looked familiar, but couldn't make out many of her features.

The mystery woman looked around before she made her next statement. In a lowered voice she whispered to Amy Poole, "I've heard one of the lawyers at Brady is setting her up."

Amy Poole gasped, as she replied, "Setting her up, how?"

"He's making her think he's in love with her. Wining and dining her so she'll convince everybody to vote in his favor."

"No way, I don't think she would ever do that."

Then the mystery woman grabbed one of Amy Poole's arms. "Wait, I bet before long she won't ask all of you to show up at the meetings. She won't be working as hard against them."

"Why would she do that? She needs her job. If we stop fighting she won't have a job either."

The woman stopped talking for a moment. From where LaKia sat she could tell the woman searched for an answer. Then suddenly, she blurted out, "She has another job offer."

The news made Amy Poole grab the sink she stood beside. "She has another job. So, she doesn't care what happens to us."

"No." The two women began to walk towards the bathroom door. The mystery woman said, "You watch and see if what I'm telling you isn't true."

"Everybody needs to know," said Amy Poole as the two women walked out of the bathroom.

Amy Poole's words were the last thing she heard before the stall beside her flushed. But, she swore the mystery woman paused at the door and glanced back at the stall where she hid.

How could she be such a fool?

That's why they smiled in her face. They marveled at Kendis' work. They were congratulating him on his ability to fool her so easily. A game! The calls, the dinners, the talks, as she stood over the sink staring into the mirror the next thought made her feel sick...the sex!

He lied to her.

Bastard. He knew more about her than any man. His promises had meant nothing. This whole thing about needing to protect her was a lie. He hadn't taken her into his confidence...it was part of his bigger plan.

Walking out of the bathroom, she passed by Amy Poole, but she didn't speak. Amy had already begun to gossip with the other merchants.

Before the end of the day everyone, including her bosses, would be well informed.

The images on the television became one big fuzzy rainbow of color to LaKia as she gazed into it for answers to the questions in her head. Too late to call Nichelle. She didn't want to worry her Mom. Dad.

The clang of the wine glass against the glass table startled her. As she pondered what to do, she flipped the gold bracelet she wore around her wrist.

Her father passed away of colon cancer just before she went away to college. He never liked doctors. When he was a young boy, his mother had died of breast cancer. No matter how much she begged him to have surgery, he refused.

Confused with tears streaming down her face, she picked up the phone and dialed.

"Hello."

DeWayne's calm voice soothed her thoughts.

"Hey...Baby Bro."

"Hey Sis, what's up?"

She steadied her trembling words. "Nothing much, just wanted to give you a yell. What you up to?"

"Cooking. You know me. I closed the restaurant a few hours early. Thought I'd come home and make something special for baby girl and me."

LaKia admired her younger brother. He never let anything stop him. He knew what he wanted and he went after it. Instead of going to college at nineteen he moved to San Francisco, California where he attended one of the top culinary schools. After school, he stayed and worked in some of the best restaurants San Francisco. During his six years there, he met a woman he loved. But, life isn't always fair. She died during childbirth. DeWayne moved back to Arkansas with his daughter, Taylor.

Last year, LaKia loaned him money to help him start his own restaurant, Southern Stylz. This year he expanded by adding a cable cooking show. And his new love worked with him every day.

"So, what are you cooking?" She could hear the bang of pots and pans in the background.

"Pork tenderloin with a fig sauce."

"Figs, I thought you swore off figs for life at eight."

"Yeah, but that was your fault, Sis. How are you gonna let your little brother pick every fig off of the tree and stuff it in his mouth."

"Hey, who wants their little bratty brother following around after them all day? Besides, I didn't know you would eat all of them."

"And Dad made me promise not to tell Ma."

"Can you imagine? She would've been so worried. She probably would've walked all of the way from work."

"This time, I'm only using a few not a whole tree."

"Well, it sounds good. I think I can smell it through the phone."

With a hearty laugh, he said, "I hope the people watching my cable show can smell it, too." He paused. "So, are you going to tell me why you really called?"

"What, I've got to have a reason to call?"

"Naw, but you can't hide the sound in your voice, Sis."

She could never hide much from him.

With a heavy sigh, she said, "It's Kendis."

"Kendis?"

"Yeah. Today, I heard he's playing me. That he's not in love with me, but using me to help him with all of this stuff going on with the development."

"You heard it? Where did you hear it? From him?"

Unable to hold back the tears any longer. She cried as she told her brother how she hid in the stall of the bathroom and listened to the two women discuss Kendis' plan.

"Sis, why didn't you walk out of the stall and ask them how they found out? For all you know they could be lying. Maybe they knew you were in there."

She thought about what he said, but then she shook it off. How would they have known she was in there? What were they doing watching her? Besides, although the other woman looked vaguely familiar, she couldn't place her.

"Why would they stand there and make up a lie like that?"

"I don't know. I've never met the man, but from what you've told me, maybe you should just ask him about it. See what he says."

"But if I ask him, that gives him the chance to lie to me again."

"So, you'd rather listen to two gossipy chicks in a bathroom instead of your man?"

OK, so when did my baby brother become so grown up? "I don't know. There's so much at stake."

"All I know is that if he loves you what you heard isn't true. If you love him, you should give him the chance to clear everything up."

After hours of laughter and tears, she stretched out on her couch, and pulled her blanket up around her chin as she dozed off.

Friday came quick—too quick for LaKia. Browsing through the department store with Nichelle for a dress to wear to the dinner party with Kendis later that night seemed surreal. She had changed her mind a million times over the last week, but finally decided to go. It would be the perfect time to separate gossip from truth.

Deflecting accusations from her merchants about her loyalty to them verses Kendis, over the last week, had been difficult. She'd put a lot of hours into stopping Eastover's development. Their lack of trust wounded her and negatively influenced her ability to do her job.

Kendis' actions had hurt her personally and professionally.

She was determined to do as her brother had suggested and find the truth. She'd avoided Kendis all week. But, as her mind wandered, she could feel his arms around her—caressing her body.

What should she do? Should she let him come over make love to her, and tell her everything she wanted to hear when it all could be a lie?

No.

She kept her distance until she could decide for herself what was really going on.

Holding a white dress in the air, Nichelle asked, "What about this one?"

"Huh?" She wasn't ignoring her, but her thoughts kept running away with her. Spinning around she awed at the simple white dress Nichelle held in the air. Beautiful. The fabric flowed back and forth with every move of her friend's hand.

She traced the rhinestones sewn into the straps with her fingers.

"I love it. These beads on the straps are gorgeous."

"Yep."

She knew what Nichelle thought without her saying a word. It's not a wedding dress. And the way things were going, it would never turn into one.

"Nichelle, it's not a wedding dress. It's a cocktail dress."

"Today cocktail dress with the boss, tomorrow, wedding dress with the family."

"Oh my God, you will never give up."

"Why should I? You deserve this. He's a good guy."

"I guess." She sucked her teeth sarcastically.

A haze of confusion drifted across Nichelle's face.

Taking the dress, she bumped into three racks of clothes as she ran into the fitting room to break away from

Nichelle's glance. She knew she'd acted irrationally—like a high school brat.

The beads on the spaghetti shoulder straps sparkled against her skin, guiding whoever might be looking from the snuggly fit silk fabric along her bust-line down her back where the two straps crossed before blending back into the fabric of the dress which tastefully hugged her slightly bowed hips and round bottom. The dress stopped just below her knees showing off her long legs. She knew the perfect pair of shoes to wear. They were beaded with the same rhinestones. Without showing the dress to Nichelle as she normally would. She carefully removed it and placed it back on its hanger.

Regardless of what happened tonight, she was going to look damn good.

While waiting in line to pay for the dress, Nichelle didn't say anything. That wasn't normal. LaKia was certain she would say something as soon as she walked out of the dressing room, but she didn't. They stopped in the food court and grabbed some bourbon chicken, one of her favorites, but still Nichelle didn't say anything.

As she carefully placed the dress into the trunk of her car, it hit her like a ton of bricks had fallen on her head. Nichelle knew something. What does she know? Why would Nichelle keep a secret from her? She was her best friend. She wouldn't keep some horrible secret from her would she?

LaKia dropped heavily into the driver's seat next to Nichelle. "What do you know about Kendis and the rumors?"

Nichelle's sad expression immediately made her regret her accusation, but it was too late to take the words back.

"I don't know what you're talking about," responded Nichelle sadly.

"You've got to know something. Terrence is his best friend and your husband."

"So?"

LaKia grew angrier as she thought about Kendis and his tricks. She wanted to yell and scream at somebody. But, Nichelle sat across from her with a doe-like expression on her face. Maybe, she didn't have the answers.

"If you don't know what I'm talking about, why haven't you said anything all day?"

"I didn't know what to say because I didn't know what you were talking about."

She could feel her cheeks redden. "Rumors have been floating around at work."

"What rumors?"

Slowly LaKia told Nichelle about the rumors. When she finished she waited silently for Nichelle to say something.

"And the other day, my boss calls me into his office to ask me about them."

"What?"

"I told him there was nothing to them. Yes, we'd been dating, but I would take care of everything. He said he would wait to hear from me before he did anything, but I can't believe how easy everyone seems to believe the worse. After all of my work. They've had two meetings this week that I haven't been involved in."

"What. You've been working your ass off. Have you told Kendis?"

"Why?" She was perturbed at the question. Nichelle's remark was almost a carbon copy of her brother's.

Was she the only one that doubted Kendis' sincerity?

Peering out of the corner of her eye at LaKia, Nichelle said, "Because there must be something we don't know."

"Why do you say that? Remember, they told us his company wanted him to do something he wasn't happy with.

Maybe this is it. There's something going on that we don't know."

Briefly, LaKia took comfort in Nichelle's words.

"But if that's the case, then who was the woman feeding all of the information to Amy Poole."

"I don't know, but Kendis might."

LaKia slowed the car down to hand the parking garage attendant her ticket to exit.

"We should talk to Terrence."

"No, not yet. I want to talk to Kendis first," said LaKia with a hint of panic in her voice.

"How long has this been going on?"

LaKia read the flashing red electronic display in front of her. Her total was $15.00. Nichelle handed her a twenty. LaKia gave the money to the attendant and waited for the change. Handing the change back to Nichelle, she said, "About a week."

Nichelle's voice rose slightly as she said, "You've known that long and didn't say anything to me? Why?"

LaKia focused on the road signs leading her from Virginia back to Maryland. "I wasn't sure what I was going to do."

"Now, you know what you're going to do?"

"No. I've been going back and forth trying to decide."

Holding her cell phone in her hand, Nichelle asked, "Why don't you want me to ask Terrence? If Kendis is up to something, Terrence would know."

Shame choking back her words, LaKia responded, "What if Terrence knows, but won't tell us?"

LaKia didn't look at her friend because she knew if she did she would see disappointment on her face. Nichelle loved her, but she was convinced she'd take her chances with a heavy weight boxer for Terrence.

Nichelle's brows furrowed deeply. "If he knows anything more than what he told me, then I trust his decision. But, how will we know if we don't ask."

"Tonight at the dinner I was going to talk to Kendis. Wait until then that'll give me the chance to make sure he doesn't have time to make up anything."

A guarded smile broke out across Nichelle's face as she said, "Okay, our own little secret mission." She continued in a whispered voice, "Agent 007 reporting for duty."

LaKia couldn't stop herself from giggling. For over a week, she worried herself over whether or not Kendis loved her. Had he lied to her? Was he still lying to her? In a matter of moments Nichelle had managed to make her laugh. She couldn't remember the last time she had laughed.

When she dropped Nichelle off, she reminded her not to tell Terrence anything until after her dinner with Kendis. That should give her enough time.

"Nichelle, you've got to promise me. This is important."

"Promise."

Driving home took LaKia nearly an hour. As she twisted the key in the lock, she looked forward to lounging in a bath with a drink before dinner.

"Crap." LaKia snapped the fingers on her right hand as the words escaped her. In a daze, she'd left the dress in the trunk of her car. Removing the key from her front door, she walked back to her car.

As she trudged up the stairs, the dress felt as heavy as her heart. She didn't know how the evening would end, but she was determined to go through with her plan.

Soaking in the bathtub, LaKia sipped on a glass of wine as she mulled over her plan for the night. Placing the glass on the rim of her Jacuzzi tub, she rested her head on an inflatable pillow. She hummed to the music traveling through the walls of the condo from her bedroom as it lulled her off to sleep. When she woke she didn't feel like rushing out of the tub, but the bubbles on top of the water had thinned and the water had chilled.

As she dried her skin, she tugged at its prune-like texture. She had a lot to do to prepare for her night of discovery and intrigue, and she didn't have much time before Kendis arrived.

After smothering her body in aloe vera and dusting it with a light floral scented powder, she slipped the dress over her head. Combing through her hair, she loosened the curls until nothing but deep auburn waves remained.

She couldn't resist admiring herself in the floor-length mirror hanging from her closet door. The dress accentuated every curve of her body tastefully. The open-toed, clear, beaded sandals perfectly displayed her French-manicured toes. As she shifted her position to see all sides of herself in the mirror the silk fabric of the dress brushed across her skin like Kendis' soft, warm breath.

Kendis would love it.

Moments later, Kendis knocked at her door.

Showtime!

CHAPTER ELEVEN

The silence in the SUV enveloped them as Kendis drove to Carl's house. The past week had been lonely without LaKia. Each time he called her recorded voice asked him to leave a message. During council meetings he rarely had an idle moment to spare. But, when he did catch her, she avoided him at every turn.

Everything he had stood in limbo because of his love for her. He knew this game would take its toll on their relationship.

They rode in unbearable silence.

"LaKia, what's up?"

"What do you mean?"

Keeping his eyes on the road he tightened his grip on the wheel. "I haven't seen you in damn near a week. I thought we were doing something here. You're running from me again. Why?"

There's no way she could still be pissed because she didn't know his full plan. It protected her.

Eyeing him skeptically, she folded her arms across her body. "What did you think we were doing?"

Pulling the SUV over to the side of the road, Kendis turned his hazard lights on and put the car in park.

"Listen, we don't have to go if you don't want to."

With a look of disbelief, she said, "Really?"

"Really. We could go back to my place I could cook, we could talk or we could go out to dinner. Tell me what you want?"

His words didn't sway her. Still, she sat tight in the corner of her seat. Distant and waiting.

"I want to go to the dinner party."

It made no sense to argue. A lovey dovey couple would be better for his game, but he'd figure out a way to make it work. He gave up and put the car back in route to Carl's.

"Okay."

Arriving at the gated community in Bethesda, MD, he turned toward her and said, "If you feel uncomfortable or want to leave at any time, let me know and we can roll out."

"I'll let you know."

Mingling with a bunch of parasites made Kendis feel dirty. The smiles and pats on the back began to annoy the hell out of him after the first five minutes. If LaKia wasn't so pissed at least he could pretend to be somewhere else. Have a little fun. As much as possible, he kept her at his side. The idiots in the room could tell her something that might confuse her more.

He threw the drink he held back to calm the anger rising as he watched Larry slither up next to her when she exited the bathroom. He didn't know what Larry wanted to say, but he knew he didn't want him near her. He leapt from his seat to her side in long strides. His presence cut the conversation short. Larry walked away after politely saying, "Hello." There was no need for him to respond.

"You ready?"

"No, we've barely spoken to anyone. Why did you run over here when you saw Larry?"

"If you're riding with me, let's go." He turned to walk away. "I'm ready to go."

"Why, are you tired?"

"No, but..."

"But what?"

Taking hold of her hand, he moved her away from the crowd as much as he could. He slipped into a small alcove sheltered by a large potted tree.

The nearness of her body to his didn't help. Too many days had passed since he'd held her. Damn, the air conditioner blew the fragrance of her shampoo straight at him. He couldn't stop himself from remembering the last time he'd smelled it all over him. "We need to talk, let's go."

LaKia had a lot to say. She refused to be kept in the dark any longer. As she rode beside him, she searched for the right words. But, she couldn't find them. "Why in the hell are you spreading rumors about me? You should've told me that was part of your secret plan."

"What rumors?"

Kendis' cell phone rang. After glancing at the LCD display, he said, "Its Terrence, he's been calling all night. I'll call him back. What rumors?"

"Everybody at my mall is talking about how I'm being made a fool of by you. That you're using me to influence them."

Frustrated with her lack of self-control, tears streamed down her cheeks gathering at her chin where they dripped to the silk fabric covering her bust. She'd struggled with her emotions throughout the night scurrying out of sight to the bathroom whenever she felt tears welling up.

But, trapped in Kendis' car, she couldn't stop.

GIVE ME EVERYTHING

Kendis pulled the car into the parking lot of an all-night diner. The fluorescent white and green sign hanging from the building provided the only light against the darkness of the night sky.

"It's not true, LaKia."

He used his fingers to brush away her tears, but they fell faster than he could catch them.

Between tearful sniffs, she asked, "Then what's going on?"

Staring into Kendis' eyes as she waited on an answer, LaKia couldn't control her fears. She yearned to lay her head against his chest and have his heartbeat send her off to sleep. God, she missed the feel of his fingers as he combed through her hair while he watched television. Were the months they'd spent together a fantasy or a lie?

"Remember that town council meeting a while ago when you and I sat out in the gazebo talking?" he finally asked.

"Yes."

"Larry saw us and he told Carl. The two of them concocted the idea of...of me making you fall in love with me to help us win over your tenants. They offered me a big bonus if I helped."

"So, that's why..."

Kendis cut off her words.

"No, that's not why anything."

He reached for her hands, but she opened the passenger door and jumped out of the car. She didn't want him to touch her.

Or, maybe, she did want his touch. Too much. As she walked away, she missed the touch of his mouth against hers.

She shivered as she remembered the feel of his breath across her skin.

She heard a car door close behind her. "LaKia, baby, I'm in love with you. You know that. I never planned on doing any of what they asked. I needed time. We talked about this. I couldn't tell you everything to protect you."

She'd left her jacket in the seat. Wrapping her arms around her body, she rubbed her hands up and down her arms as she spun and stared into his chest. She stepped back. "You needed time for what?"

"To find another job and get enough on tape to protect myself."

Find another job? The crippling pain that hit LaKia in her stomach made her flinch. She didn't want that to be true either. Nichelle told her she would need to deal with it when it came, and now it was here, but she didn't know how to deal with it. Too much, too fast.

He extended his arm to LaKia. "Please come back to the car. This lot is dark." He wrapped his jacket around her shoulders.

LaKia scanned the lot. He was right. There were only a few cars parked aside from his truck. She could see people in the restaurant pointing as they stared at them through the bay windows.

"I've received a few job offers. I wanted to tell you, but Terrence and I both thought it might be best if we didn't tell you or Nichelle too much, because we needed you two to make it real for everybody. And I still don't have quite enough on tape, yet."

Cautiously returning to the car, LaKia asked, "Who did you send from your office to my mall to tell Amy Poole you were just stringing me along?"

"Amy Poole, who's that?"

"Amy Poole, she's a merchant in my mall. I heard her and another woman talking about all of this in the bathroom."

"Who was the other woman?"

"I don't know, she wasn't from my mall, I assumed she was from your company."

"What did she look like?"

"Tall, light-skinned, long black hair."

"I can't believe they would do that shit."

"What?" Lakia asked.

"Remember my ex, Kim?" He banged his fist against the steering wheel. "Damn. So, that's the source."

Kim. She never thought she'd ever forget her.

"But why would she get involved?"

"Because baby."

"Because, what?"

The bolt from the blue that struck LaKia brought a nervous smile to her face as she got back into the car with Kendis closing the door behind her.

After he sat, she said, "Because you're in love with me and she wants you back."

This time Kendis didn't have to ask, she kissed him. She swore she heard the sound of her heartbeat increase with each touch of his lips. Too much time had passed and her body wanted to catch up. The bucket seats and lack of privacy did not help her.

He broke their embrace.

"Baby, they needed to discredit you. I'm so sorry; I don't know how she got involved. I don't know how this got so big."

"We're talking about a lot of money Kendis."

"I know, but I don't care. I'm in love with you and I don't want to be the reason you lose your job or damage your career."

"I can take care of myself don't worry." She thought for a moment. "The reason I was so upset was not just because of my job, but because I felt like you'd lied to me about everything."

"I'm sorry, baby."

"No, I'm sorry. I should've trusted you. But...I guess I still look for men to hurt me. To take what they want without really caring."

"Baby, we've both been through a lot, but I'm in love with you. This will be wrapped up soon and your reputation will be okay."

As Kendis started up the truck, she fastened her seatbelt.

"So, what do we do now?"

"I don't know, but whatever it is, it needs to include me kicking Larry Dukes' ass."

LaKia sat in the middle of the food court surrounded by the smells of pretzels, hot dogs, ice cream, fried chicken and burgers, but she couldn't eat any of it. Shoppers smiled and waved as they walked past her. Moms with their strollers and senior citizens with their walkers wore mall walker t-shirts with pride as they looped around the mall for their routine workout. Sticky fingered children licked ice cream from their hands with smiles drew her attention.

Amy Poole approached her table. She pulled one of the small blue metal chairs from the table and sat.

"LaKia, some of the merchants want to know if you will be at the next council meeting. It's our last chance to stop Eastover."

"Of course, why wouldn't I be there?"

"I don't know. We've been hearing a lot of things."

"Like what?"

Amy didn't elaborate. Instead, she stared into the distance over LaKia's right shoulder.

LaKia glanced over her shoulder to see what Amy Poole focused on. For a few seconds, she saw her, Kim, before her figure in the distance dipped behind a mall directory.

"Amy, what have you been hearing?"

"Well, someone's been telling us you aren't trying to help us. That you are working for Eastover...at least for one of the lawyers at Eastover."

Annoyed, LaKia locked her eyes onto Amy's.

"Who told you that?"

"I don't want to spread rumors. I don't want to get anyone in trouble."

No one but me.

Collecting her trash, LaKia pushed away from the table. "Don't worry about any rumors. Everything will be cleared up at the next council meeting."

Amy, the other merchants, and her bosses questioned her loyalty. But, she still loved her job. Kendis sat on the brink of giving up everything for her. The full weight of it hadn't hit her over the weekend, but now it hit her hard. He loved her.

Blinded by her own emotions, she raced from the packed food court to her office. The crowd of merchants gathered at her boss's office grabbed her attention. But, she needed to be alone for a moment.

"LaKia."

Crap. "Yes?"

"Can we talk?" asked Jack Diehl, the President of Diehl Realty Group. The number of times she'd seen him in the office over the years could be counted on one hand. He and Kim on the same day couldn't be a good thing.

"Sure."

"Have a seat."

LaKia slid one of the overpriced leather sling back chairs away from the conference table and sat.

"Have you been able to get a handle on these rumors?"

"Not yet, Jack. But I know how they began and I'm working on it."

"The ladies out there were telling me about some of the latest. It's not looking good at all."

"I know, sir, but trust me none of it is true."

"I've worked with you for how many years, now? Four or five. I know they aren't true, but this can't continue. I'll have to make some decisions soon. Is there anything I can do to help you resolve this?"

"No, sir. I was on my way to my office to take care of it right now."

"Okay, don't let me stop you."

As she left his office, she knew she had to do something quick. She shut her door behind her with such force the frame around it rattled. What was she going to do? She had to help him even if that meant losing him. But, how?

Kendis' mind pondered his last night with LaKia as he rushed down the hallway to his weekly meeting with Carl. All weekend he tried to forget and shake off the look in her eyes Friday, but he couldn't. He'd damn near begged her to let him stay the night, but she refused. Once again they were taking a step back, when he wanted to move forward.

He wanted to marry her. Have a real family.

He clicked the record button on his tape recorder as he turned the corner, his face bounced off something soft and shiny. Six red Mylar balloons attached to a clear glass vase containing a dozen white roses.

The grin on his assistant's face nearly blinded him as she loudly broadcasted, "These are from LaKia."

Everyone waiting in the conference room shifted in their chairs to see.

Removing the card from the flowers, Kendis said, "Please place them in my office."

The mention of LaKia's name had changed everything. He wanted to read the card, but he knew the flowers were a signal. She was going to help him.

He sat at the conference table ready for whatever dumb ass thing they had to say.

Carl began and ended the conversation.

At the conclusion of the meeting, knew he finally had what he needed. He and Terrence had reviewed the tapes he'd made over the past weeks, and until now, they didn't think he had enough to save his ass if he showed his hand anytime soon. He'd needed more.

As he rose from the conference table to head back to his office, Carl said, "Wait Kendis."

Of course his sidekick Larry stood at his side. Larry didn't have the balls to confront him without Carl or some other witness.

"I noticed LaKia enjoyed herself at the dinner party."

Kendis tried to stifle a smile as he sat back down at the table. The tiny rollers inside the small recorder vibrated against his chest.

"I think she did Carl."

"How is everything going with our little endeavor?"

He needed Carl to elaborate. Most of his tapes were of Larry. They would definitely end Larry's career, but he wanted Carl, too. Carl would let Larry be the scapegoat and Kendis would be panhandling on the corner for dinner.

"Our endeavor?"

Carl FitzSimmons regarded Kendis cautiously, exchanging a questioning glance with Larry. Larry chimed, "Do we have to spell it out for you? My source tells me it looks like things are going our way. Do you think merchants are ready to deal?"

Kendis asked, "Exactly what is the next phase? What is the deal? You haven't told me much lately." Larry kept talking, but Carl watched Kendis carefully saying nothing.

"Have you asked her to question her merchants? See which ones might want to move to our property or help us out with the council," Larry persisted.

Why in the hell wasn't Carl talking?

From Carl's body language, Kendis knew he was suspicious. Maybe, if he looked more relaxed he could get more from Carl. He needed them both on tape to protect his ass.

Removing his suit jacket, he placed it on a chair closer to Carl FitzSimmons. "Look Larry, this takes time. I can't invite her to a dinner party one night, sleep with her the next and presto it's a done deal."

"Kendis relax," said Carl. "We're just wondering when we can move on with this project. It's critical to our being able to move forward with Eastover and get this contract signed. The next council meeting will be soon. Those signatures could help us push this through."

"I'm working on it, but like I said before...she and I were not any sort of a couple. Getting her to trust me has been tough."

Carl nodded at the card Kendis plucked from the roses peeping out of his shirt pocket. "I can see you are working on that."

Tapping the card with a finger, Kendis said, "Exactly."

Fidgeting in his seat, Larry Dukes said, "When do you think you would be able close?"

"Soon, the next town council meeting will be in about two weeks, I think I can get something from her by then."

Carl had a reserved smile on his face, "O.K., I think we can work with that. With you and Larry's insider, we can have some names before the council meeting."

Idling in front of Kendis' house, LaKia couldn't decide if she should stay or leave. She shook off the thought of Kim standing in his doorway in his underwear. Before she left work, she checked with the florist and they had delivered her flowers—late. But, the time didn't matter, just the affect.

Turning the volume up on the radio, she decided to stay. If she and Kendis were successful, he'd take another job and be gone...soon. Would she be able to drive there? Would she have to fly? Would he want a long-distance relationship? Her head began to throb. Massaging her temples she thought maybe she'd go around the corner to the grocery store and pick up some aspirin.

She could call Kendis to see when he would make it home while she drove to the store. Checking her rearview mirror as she backed down the driveway, she flipped open her cell phone, and pressed three on the speed dial for Kendis. Lights reflecting off her rearview mirror blinded her. She slammed on her brakes. Something hit the back of her car.

Before she could open the door to get out and check her damage, Kendis had sprinted to her side. "Baby, are you okay?"

"Yeah."

Kendis' face looked troubled as he asked, "You sure?"

"Yes, yes. Don't worry. I barely felt it."

"I didn't realize you were moving."

She snuggled up against his chest. "I'm okay."

Standing in front of him with his arms around her she wanted to cry. She didn't want him to go away. She didn't want to lose him. A man that would give up everything he had for her. A man willing to lose everything to protect her, not hurt her. How could she let him walk out of her life without letting him know she loved him?

She had never said those words to him.

With total abandon she threw the words into the air.

"I love you."

His arms tightened around her waist. "I love you, too."

He pressed her back against her car, and leaned his body along hers. His chest, solid and firm, pressed against her breasts as she stood on her tiptoes. If Kim watched, let her take notes. Kendis loved her and she loved him. He lowered his head to hers and she kissed him. Only hours had passed since she last kissed him, but the way her body awoke at his touch made the time feel too long. How would she be able to go without his touch when he left? She wanted to remember every cut of his body. Her tongue ran across his lips. Then softly she kissed him. His lips parted slightly, and she felt his warm breath against her lips. Longingly, her hands caressed every muscle of his back. She gripped his butt, and pulled him into her.

"LaKia, baby, wait." He stepped out of her embrace.

"Wait, huh?"

"Baby, we're outside. Let's check out the car, and go inside. We can finish this then," said Kendis with a devilish smile. He pulled her away from the car, and draped his arm over her shoulder.

With a kiss on the cheek, she agreed. "Okay."

Investigating the damage to their cars, Kendis smiled down at LaKia who nestled snuggly underneath his arm. "So, being in love with you is dangerous, huh?"

Gazing up into his eyes, she responded, "Are you scared?"

He tightened his grip around her shoulders and kissed the top of her head. "No."

There wasn't much that could be done about the cars tonight. The damage to his car didn't need any repair...maybe a little buffing. But, hers needed to go to the shop. In the morning, he would take her to the body shop around the corner to drop her car off and take her to work.

Tonight, he would make love to her until she fell asleep.

Flipping the steak he'd thrown on the range top grill for himself, he said, "They loved your roses."

Kendis watched as she removed her shoes before she sank into the big overstuffed couch he'd recently purchased. "I thought they would."

Moving as aptly as a chef, he sprinkled soy sauce over stir-fried rice. "They kept asking me when I thought I would be able to close this deal."

Laughing at the words, LaKia said, "Close this deal. So, is that what I am to you?"

She sat curled up underneath a blanket he had given her earlier. Looking at her through the pass through, he set the soy sauce on the counter and walked toward her. When he reached her, he scooped her up into his arms.

"You've never been any sort of deal to me."

She locked her arms around his neck, and rested them on his shoulders as she dropped her legs to the floor. He pulled her in so close to his body he could feel the rise and fall of her chest with each breath she took.

Parting his lips, he covered her top lip with his mouth briefly before focusing on her bottom. She opened her mouth allowing his tongue to explore hers, their tongues wrestled until he could feel his manhood bursting through the basketball shorts he had changed into.

Her body yielded in his arms, which signaled to him she was keen for whatever he wanted next.

He wanted her.

The shrill sound from the smoke detector drew his attention. He didn't smell the meat on the grill burn.

Softly, she whispered into his ear, "I guess we'll be ordering pizza."

He kissed her softly, then he said, "Wait one minute." Dashing over to the kitchen, he shut off the grill. Before she lowered her arms, he was back beneath them guiding her gently into the cushions of the couch.

He stretched her body along the length of the couch, lowering his down on top of hers. Running his hand along her body, he said, "Tonight, I want us to take our time."

"Take our time?"

"I want to see and know all of you. I don't want to forget a thing."

Slowly rising from the couch, LaKia stood in front of Kendis and began to remove her clothing. He mirrored her actions and removed a piece of clothing with each piece she discarded to the floor.

He didn't have as much to take off as she did. Before long, he was naked. But parts of her were still clad from his sight by a pink panty set. Her nearly naked body caused his body to ache. As she stood in front of him considering her next move, he thought he would lose control. When she unsnapped her bra, her breasts bounced then stilled, and sat high and perfect on her chest. Her nipples were erect waiting for his mouth.

When she reached for her panties, her movement stalled. She teased him. He knew it. Covering his rod with a condom from his pocket, he stroked himself slowly as he watched her. If she didn't pull the panties off, he would rip them off.

He couldn't wait any longer, reaching for her pink thongs; he helped her get rid of them. He pulled her into his lap placing one of her long legs on either side of his thighs.

The moan she released when he slid inside of her encouraged him to thrust deeper. Rhythmically their bodies clapped as he pushed and pulled. With each thrust, her body writhed more.

Rising from the couch, standing to his full height, he bounced LaKia up and down against his thighs. He couldn't hold on for long; the sensation of her body slapping into his caused him to release. Her kisses deepened as he lowered her to the couch, he said, "Are you okay."

Arching her back, pushed her breasts higher into the air towards him, she stretched her body out and purred, "Of course."

He couldn't take his eyes off her as she wriggled her body against the soft cushions of the couch.

His body stiffened again.

Covering her nipple with his mouth he sucked hard, playfully moving his tongue back and forth around it until he could feel it harden in his mouth. Using his fingers he massaged her clit until her body moved with his hand.

Shifting to the floor, he stretched out on his back and pulled her body down to meet his. She took the lead; he followed. This time she reached for the condom. Then, she placed all of him inside of her, as she slid her body down over his her lips parted tempting him. Slowly, she moved her pelvis back and forth until he couldn't take it. He grabbed her bottom to control her movements, and bounced her up and down at a faster harder pace.

Damn. Each time he brought her body down to his, he tried to thrust his own as deep as possible. She threw her head back and dug her nails into his chest. He grabbed her butt with both hands and held her body against his. The feeling of her warmth around him took over. What would he do without her in his life?

CHAPTER TWELVE

Today, Carl wouldn't be at the office much longer, he'd planned a victory trip to Portofino, Italy. He and LaKia had given him a list of fake signatures and convinced him and Larry everything was okay.

If Kendis intended to put his tape to the test, he had to do it now. He had to confront Carl and Larry because Larry wouldn't have the authority to make the approvals he needed. Kendis examined the docs he had in the envelope again. The papers looked exactly the same as they had moments ago.

Kendis examined the reception area outside of Carl's office while he waited for the okay signal from Carl's secretary to enter.

Mahogany.

Everything around him was mahogany, over-sized antique furniture. It would probably take five men his size to move just one piece. Law books, mostly for show, he couldn't recall one time when he'd seen anyone using them, but there they were. Hundreds of them.

He thought he would practice law forever. But, as if staring into a crystal ball, his future played out clearly in his daydreams. LaKia and a family with her were what he wanted. Children.

Barking at Kendis, Carl beckoned him. "Kendis come on in. Sit down."

Before Kendis could say anything the phone rang. Quickly Carl threw up the index finger on his right hand signaling for Kendis to wait a moment while he answered the phone. Kendis knew by Carl's responses that Larry was on the other end. Perfect. Carl concluded by telling the caller to join them. Moments later, Larry appeared in the doorway.

Kendis handed Carl the envelope he'd held so protectively. Without saying a word, Kendis revealed a small tape recorder hidden in his inside right jacket pocket. Sitting it on Carl's desk, he pushed play. Carl's normally olive complexion gradually darkened into a deep shade of crimson as the tape played. Larry Dukes had developed a little twitch at the left corner of his mouth.

Picking the tape recorder up off the desk, Kendis stood to leave.

"Carl, I am a team player, but not for your team. You hired the wrong person for this job. I fell in love with her."

"Kendis, you just fucked up your career...you know that?" said Carl.

Larry snickered at Carl's comment.

Halting at the door, Kendis turned to face Carl and Larry shaking the tape recorder for them both to see. "Don't fuck with her...or me again. This can stay between us or it can go public. I've got more of these. This was just a little to let you know I had it."

Anger showed in Carl's eyes as he pushed away from his desk and walked in Kendis' direction. Nose to nose they stood. Carl's girth filled the doorway. Larry watched from a coward's distance.

"Do you think you can threaten me with a tape?"

"I know I can. How do you think the partners will feel when they find out you're the reason they lost millions?" Pointing to Larry, he said, "What? You going to make that idiot the scapegoat? That won't work because I've got your voice, too."

Larry said, "What me? Scapegoat?"

Kendis laughed. "Who do you think? You're a damn fool. If they can't take me down, the next person is you."

Larry gasped. "What?"

"Shut up, Larry," said Carl.

"Carl, I'll be expecting your letter of recommendation to be forwarded to me at the address I left with your secretary. Everything in the packet should be pretty clear."

Kendis glanced at Carl's secretary. She pretended to be occupied by whatever was on her computer screen.

He locked his eyes on Larry. Larry shifted his weight from one foot to the other, but he wasn't able to shake the hold Kendis had on him. Lowering his voice to a guttural growl, he said, "Larry, next time be sure you have the right woman working for you."

Kendis strolled down the corridor to his corner office with Carl and Larry whispering angrily at his back.

Reflecting on his day as he sat in the city council boardroom, Kendis chuckled at Larry's periodic checks throughout the day, he'd stuck his head into Kendis' office for re-assurance about LaKia. Silently nodding his head in agreement with whatever Larry said Kendis never showed Larry any other sign of acknowledgment. That is not until he walked into Carl's office.

Observing Larry from his normal position beside him at the front table, Kendis marveled at how the buttons on Larry's shirt stretched to hold the two pieces of fabric together. The next breath he took would make them pop Kendis was certain as he watched him begin his speech.

GIVE ME EVERYTHING

"Honorable Mayor and council members at this time I would like to remove Eastover's bid for development."

The room stirred with the conclusion of his comments. Reporters jotted hurriedly on their pads, protesters jeered and clapped with success, and supporters gasped collectively in disappointment.

Shocked, the Mayor asked, "Is there a reason for your sudden change of mind?"

"Madame Mayor we've reconsidered the concerns of the environmentalists and the city. Also, without the support of the city with highway construction costs we believe the costs of development would put us over planned budget considerably."

Kendis knew the Mayor would believe Larry's rationale because they'd been fighting with those issues the entire life of the project.

Glancing over the room, he was glad to see LaKia had kept her promise. Everyone from her mall was there including Amy. If he were a woman, he'd slap her. How could she believe Kim? LaKia had helped Amy Poole when she needed to re-model her store, but didn't have the cash. You can't trust anybody. Holding back a laugh, he realized Carl must have thought the same thing about him.

LaKia's boss, Jack, slapped her on the back and let out a hearty laugh.

"Mr. Dukes, we understand your hesitation and thank you for your consideration of this project. Maybe in the near future we will be able to come to an agreeable arrangement."

"Thank you, Mayor."

Besieged by reporters, neither Larry nor Kendis could leave the boardroom. No matter how much they questioned them, they didn't elaborate. Prepared with well-rehearsed statements, they responded to the questions asked effortlessly.

Kendis touted LaKia's efforts and noted her company's dedication to the community.

Before departing, he watched LaKia as reporters, council members, her boss, co-workers, and merchants congratulated her. Amy Poole hugged her and kissed her on the cheek.

Their eyes linked as he walked in reverse out of the door.

Three months later...

Every week since Kendis left, LaKia received a bouquet of flowers each more beautiful than the last: wildflowers, roses, sunflowers, and calla lilies—her favorite.

She couldn't keep her mind on the road because she was so excited about meeting Kendis for dinner at Windows, a linen tablecloth restaurant in the round at the top of a Baltimore hotel. He flew in so they could spend the weekend together.

Since Eastover, she had begun her own consulting agency. No matter how much she tried, it still hurt that her boss and merchants thought she could be the type of person who would betray everyone. But, business was business, and she'd received so many requests for marketing advice that she decided to give up her job and open her own marketing consulting company. Of course, this would give her enough flexibility to do whatever she wanted to do when she wanted to do it. She could travel to visit Kendis at will.

Carl had given Kendis his recommendation, and fired Larry as he'd predicted. Kendis had taken a job in Tennessee working for a small law firm. Civil Law—no longer corporate law. He and his father were a lot happier.

Walking through the restaurant behind the waiter that showed her to her table, LaKia had butterflies in her stomach. When she saw Kendis she wanted to run into his arms, but she didn't. His beautiful smile warmed her from the other side of the room.

Before Kendis, she'd been afraid, but not anymore. Now, she yearned for him. For his love.

The crisp white tablecloths surrounding Kendis contrasted against his dark skin and charcoal grey suit. He appeared to be separate from everything around him. When he hugged her, the scent of his cologne surrounded her. Vivid memories of their last night together rushed through her mind. The softness of his mouth and the firmness of his hands as they trailed up and down her body exploring every nook excited her body again.

Whispering into his ear, she said, "I've missed you."

"I've missed you, too," he said with a wanting sound in his voice.

"We can leave here now and go to my place."

"No, not yet."

All through dinner, LaKia couldn't stop thinking about taking him home and devouring him the whole night—not food.

Following Kendis back to her condo, she thought about what she would do to him when she got him alone. There were a lot of cars parked on her street. Why?

Kissing Kendis as she walked backwards into her condo, she didn't notice the crowd of people waiting inside. The sounds of laughter and clapping around her disturbed her delicious fantasies. Her mother and brother, Nichelle and Terrence, and others along with some she didn't know—who were they?

Kendis dropped down to one knee.

Tears began to stream out of LaKia's eyes as he opened the small red velvet box he held in his hand.

"Will you marry me?"

Kendis' voice trembled as he said the words he'd practiced for months.

The crowd of people with their laughs, giggles, and applause faded into the background. He watched her lips as she said, "Yes," crying audibly.

Nuzzling the side of his face into the top of her curly auburn hair, he tightened his grip around her torso. He had been leery of love, but not anymore.

Holding LaKia in his arms as she cried, Kendis couldn't believe how good it felt. Surrounded by their families, embracing the woman he loved was all he'd ever wanted.

Book Club Discussion Guide

Give Me Everything

by Angela Kay Austin

- According to a survey from 2009, the average age of men when they marry (the first time) is 28, and for women it is 26. Unlike the '50s, where the average age for men was 23, and for women 20. Do you think this is a good trend, or not?

- In 2009, 35% of women 40-49 had divorced, down from 40% in 1996. This number sounds positive, but can you think of reasons for this decline?

- Three percent of people in this same 2009 study had been married more than three times. Is there ever too many times to marry?

- An estimated one woman in eight in college is raped. In most cases the women know their attackers. What can women do to make themselves more safe, even if they're with a friend?

- Acquaintance rape is not reported as often is non-stranger rape. Why?

- Often victims of rape can develop some type of posttraumatic stress disorder. Where can they turn for help?

More Great Books
from Angela Kay Austin

 in Print and Ebook

On the Frontline
Two terrific Angela Kay Austin Short Stories For those who serve, and the ones who love them.

Scarlet's Tears – She'd lost so very much... including her sense of self, how could she go on?

Derailed – From homeless to hopeful, this young veteran builds a life she'd thought impossible. **(single also in Audiobook)**

 in Print and Ebook

Rumer

Rumer Wilson married the love of her life ten years ago, has two beautiful children, and what she believes is a wonderful life to prove it, when her world spirals into an unfamiliar place of uncertainty for everything she holds dear. Her husband falls in love with a woman hiding secrets, and the woman's brother is out for revenge.

 Also in Audiobook and Print

Sweet Victory
For her employees' sakes, Victoria James quits her job to save theirs and loses the man she thought she loved. Back to Memphis, Tennessee to a forgotten relationship with her grandfather, where everything she has is stolen. Chad Kirkpatrick, her childhood love, the first man to break her heart, now a police officer, comes to her aid. Will she put her past behind her? Will Chad forgive her?

Angela Kay Austin

Bestselling author Angela Kay Austin has expressed herself through words for as long as she can remember. Poems became songs performed with her cousin at every family gathering. But, eventually, short stories filled her favorite pink diary. An infatuation with music and theater led to years playing various instruments and small extra roles in TV shows before giving way to a degree and career in radio and TV production. After completing another degree in marketing, Angela found herself combining her love for all things creative and worked for many many years in promotions and advertising. But once again, she found herself writing, which led to her first published work which stayed on her publisher's bestseller list for ten weeks. Her second release hit the bestseller list at All Romance eBooks.

She's spoken on author panels, and served on boards for various author groups. When she's not writing, you can find her reading her favorite authors, or researching her next story idea. Angela shares her downtime with her mixed-bred rescue terrier—Midnight, in the beautiful southern state of Tennessee.

She's also a member of Romance Writers of America, From the Heart Romance Writers, Chick Lit Writers of the World, and Washington DC Romance Writers.

www.ingramcontent.com/pod-product-compliance
Lightning Source LLC
Chambersburg PA
CBHW071245130626
46556CB00003B/1174